Also by Dorothy Simpson:

SIX FEET UNDER
THE NIGHT SHE DIED
PUPPET FOR A CORPSE
CLOSE HER EYES
LAST SEEN ALIVE
DEAD ON ARRIVAL
ELEMENT OF DOUBT
SUSPICIOUS DEATH
DEAD BY MORNING
DOOMED TO DIE

HARBINGERS
OF FEAR

Dorothy Simpson

WARNER
FUTURA

A Warner Futura Book

First published in Great Britain in 1977
by Macdonald & Jane's Publishers Ltd

This edition published in 1992 by Warner Futura

ISBN 0 7474 1029 1

Phototypeset by Input Typesetting Ltd, London
Printed in Great Britain by
Cox & Wyman Ltd, Reading

Warner Futura
A Division of
Little, Brown and Company (UK) Limited
165 Great Dover Street
London SE1 4YA

For my parents

Foreword

WHEN YOU LEARN that Dorothy Simpson read Modern Languages at Bristol, was once a teacher, made her considerable mark as a Committee member of the Crime Writers' Association, and was awarded the CWA Silver Dagger in 1986, you would rightly think of her as an intellectual and expect to find that cool intellect used to good effect in novels like this. You would be right. But you would perhaps be surprised to discover deep emotions, personal cross-currents and a warm understanding of fear and frailty, existing alongside her thorough knowledge of crime and criminals.

This book, her first, was originally published in serial form in 1977, and was followed by three books which she did not publish, though characters and incidents in them, honed and refined as necessary, have been re-used in her later books. She lives in Kent and her policeman in several stories is Inspector Thanet, named not after the Greek philosophy of death, but after the Isle of Thanet area of the county!

When I reviewed one of her books on the radio, I commented on Thanet's abrasiveness towards a brilliant young musician, yet Dorothy told me her own son, in his twenties, thought the detective should be *more* abrasive. She further told me that, like other women crime writers, her male sleuth is a masculine sublimation of herself; how she would act and speak in other circumstances.

Harbingers of Fear is a suspense mystery with a puzzle and a shattering dénouement and conclusion. Unlike a Gothic story, where the heroine refuses to confide in anybody and then suffers for her independence, pregnant housewife Sarah Royd tries valiantly to confide her fears to her husband, friends, and tries to reach the police, but to no avail. No one will believe her threatened by anonymous warning cards, silent watchers, and attacks on the house itself. Masculine pooh-poohings, medical hints of pre-natal imbalance leave the distraught woman to fend for herself, to solve the mystery, nearly die in the attempt, and finally to prove the triumphant *dea ex machina* – just in time.

The tension and suspense are carefully and ominously piled up in a claustrophobic spiral of frenetic horror; just like such classic plays as *The Desperate Hours* by Joseph Hayes and *Sorry, Wrong Number* by Lucille Fletcher, where simple scenes contrast vividly with the strain and fear, simple objects can metamorphose into hidden enemies, as the screw turns relentlessly. As with those two plays, this book has a small cast of well-defined characters to increase the pace and fluency.

Mrs Simpson has a unique feel for human weaknesses and worries. Her description of the *enceinte* woman's medical problems are precise but not prolonged, acting as a catharsis for her own and her husband's emotional growth, making the reader ponder which spouse does have the major strength and will. And all readers will learn how vital it is to protect the home when, as in this book, no policeman makes even a token appearance.

JOHN KENNEDY MELLING

Chapter One

'Sarah, you're not listening.'

'Yes, I am, really.'

Alec made a sound which was something between a snort and a derisive laugh. 'Look at your plate.'

Sarah looked. The hanging lamp cast a pool of light over the débris of their supper, throwing into relief the grain and texture of the pine table and spotlighting mercilessly the neat circle of tiny balls of bread ranged around the edge of her plate, evidence of her preoccupation.

Briefly she raised her eyes to meet Alec's, levelled accusingly at her across the table. 'I'm sorry, Alec.'

'Well, what's the matter with you?'

'Nothing, really.' She tried hard to sound as though she meant it, but it was not a convincing performance. She felt very guilty. It was so unfair to Alec that, tonight of all nights, she should be inattentive, preoccupied. For months now he had been looking forward to the arrival of the Hannery Collection, and she could imagine the stir there must have been today along the sedate corridors of the County Archives Office. It was probably the most important collection of papers they had ever received on permanent loan, and Alec had been brimming over with excitement and enthusiasm when he had arrived home that evening.

'Nothing, really.' Alec's voice mimicked hers. 'Do you really think that after being married to you for six years I still can't tell when there is something the matter with you?' His voice roughened. 'What is it?'

I've bungled it, thought Sarah. Now he's hurt he won't want to listen. All the same she would have to tell him, and she glanced around the kitchen, as if for support. She loved the kitchen more than any other room in the house. To her, it was exactly what a kitchen ought to be: warm, welcoming, a place to relax in as well as work in. The sheen of natural wood, the gleam of copper, the sparkle of blue and white china usually evoked an answering glow in her, but tonight they failed her. She knew that Alec would not like what she was going to say, especially now that he was already angry with her. Alec hated mysteries, big and small. He liked everything to be clear, rational, logical, explicable.

She looked at him again, trying to gauge his reaction. His long, narrow face was still faintly flushed with excitement, his usually immaculate brown hair ruffled where he had been running his fingers through it, but her heart sank as she noted the grim expression, the brown eyes slightly dilated with anger. She floundered, trying to find words which would not antagonize him further. 'Well, it isn't really important. It's just that . . . well . . . I wondered if you'd heard of anyone finding a small white card in a pocket or handbag?'

'A small white card?' Alec stared at her blankly, clearly taken aback.

'Yes, about the size and shape of a visiting card.'

'No, I don't think so. Why?'

'Well, I found one, this morning, when I got home. In my handbag.'

She had felt tired, after shopping, and when she had parked the car as near to the front door as possible, so as to use the minimum of energy in unloading her purchases, she had switched off the ignition and sat for

2

a moment savouring the peace which surrounded her after the noise and bustle of town.

Then, clumsily – it was only four weeks until the baby was due – she had stepped out on to the tarmac and gone around to the other side of the car to take out her shopping. As the door opened, her handbag, which must have been leaning against it, fell out and most of its contents spilled on to the drive. Fortunately she had cleared it out only a few days before and there were only the bare essentials to pick up – purse, handkerchief, cheque-book, comb, lipstick, diary – and a small white card she hadn't seen before.

Alec's voice broke in impatiently. 'Well, go on, go on. What was so extraordinary about that?'

'I couldn't think how it had got there unless someone had put it there. I wondered if you had heard of anyone else getting one. You see more people than I do.'

'But why should anyone else get one? Was it advertising something?'

'No, no.' The growing exasperation on Alec's face drove her on. 'It had one of those gloomy verses from the Bible on it. The sort of thing one sees on sandwich boards. "Prepare to meet thy doom", or something.'

'Is that what it said, "Prepare to meet thy doom"?'

'No, not exactly.'

'Sarah, for God's sake get to the point. Why do I always have to drag information out of you bit by bit? What *did* it say?'

Now that they had arrived at the crux of the matter, Sarah discovered in herself an extreme reluctance to say the words aloud. She felt that by some strange alchemy they would, if spoken aloud, take on a new dimension. She was also afraid that Alec would laugh at her and ridicule her fears. But she couldn't go back now. She read the words again in her mind's eye, square printed capitals against the white background, and as she read them she said them aloud to Alec:

BOAST NOT THYSELF OF TOMORROW;
FOR THOU KNOWEST NOT WHAT A DAY
MAY BRING FORTH.
PROVERBS XXVII.1.

Alec frowned. 'Some crank, I should think. Probably some obscure religious sect. Where is it? Let me see it.'

Sarah felt an enormous surge of relief. She was suddenly conscious of a sharp pain in her hands, where her finger-nails had been digging into her palms. 'Oh, Alec, do you really think so?'

'Of course, what else could it be?'

'I'm sure you're right. It's in the sitting-room. I'll get it.'

She set off eagerly enough, but just inside the sitting-room she paused. Even now, when Alec's matter-of-fact reaction should have given her courage, she found the idea of looking at the card again thoroughly distasteful, and the prospect of touching it made her flesh crawl. All day she had studiously avoided the sitting-room, as if the small white presence had contaminated it, and the memory of its message had hovered constantly at the edge of her consciousness as she went about her work, tainting her preparations for the week-end. She had no idea why it had affected her so strongly, but ever since she had found it she had been enveloped in a mist of formless fears. She shook her head as if to clear it of these phantoms and tried to focus her thoughts on something concrete.

Firelight made monstrous leaping shapes on the rough white walls of the long low room, was reflected back at her from the small irregularly-shaped casement window on three sides of it, and was swallowed up in the shadowy recesses between the heavy oak beams which spanned the ceiling.

What a pity it was, she thought, as she had thought a thousand times before, that the furnishings did not

4

live up to the room. The flowery chintz and oak furniture were pleasant enough, but . . . uninspired. That was it. Dull, like me, thought Sarah, the familiar sense of dissatisfaction with herself welling up in her. She wasn't sufficiently sure of herself for any room she decorated to have any flair, any impact. Even the kitchen, her favourite room, had only a conventional attractiveness.

As she crossed the room and went from window to window to draw the curtains, delaying for a few moments longer the moment when she must fetch the card and show it to Alec, she remembered how, when she had been trying to decide which colour she would choose to decorate the dining-room walls, she had told him that what she would really like was to paper them in very dark green and rely upon the crisp whiteness of ceiling and woodwork to lighten the effect. 'Why don't you, then?' he had asked. She had shaken her head, dumbly. She had known why, of course – she was too much of a coward. What if it hadn't come off? What if the effect were merely dark, gloomy and heavy? She hadn't been able to risk it. What she had really wanted was for Alec to enthuse about the suggestion and adopt it, thereby lending it the weight of his authority. But he hadn't and . . .

'What on earth are you doing?' Alec's voice brought her back to the present with a guilty start. She could delay no longer.

'Just coming.'

Swiftly she crossed the room to the fireplace and reached up to take down the card from where she had stood it on the huge beam which straddled the hearth. Her hand remained arrested in mid-air. The card had gone.

She stared blankly at the place where she had put it. She distinctly remembered reaching up and standing it there. It must have fallen off. She switched on a lamp

5

and started to look about for it on the floor. There was no sign of it. She moved the coal scuttle, the log-basket, even the fire-irons, but there was nothing. She widened the area of search, moving the armchairs nearest the fire, even kneeling down and turning back the edge of the carpet, finger-nails scrabbling in haste against the tough heavy fibres, without success.

There was only one explanation, of course. It must have fallen into the fire. She stood back and tried to estimate its angle of fall. Surely it would not have fallen into the fire? The beam projected too far forward beyond the hood for that. Unless there had been a sudden draught? Had Alec opened any windows after lighting the fire?

Alec appeared in the kitchen doorway. 'Sarah? What are you doing? Can't you find it?'

'It's gone, Alec.'

'Gone?' He moved towards her, frowning. 'What do you mean, gone?'

'I put it here –' she indicated the place – 'and it's not there now.'

'Well, it must have fallen into the fire, obviously.'

'That's the point. I don't think it could have. Look, it would have fallen well in front of the hearth.'

'Not if there had been a draught.'

'Did you open any of the windows when you lit the fire?'

'You can see I didn't. I haven't been in here since then.'

'Didn't you notice the card, when you were lighting the fire?'

'No, but that doesn't necessarily mean that it wasn't there.'

'But surely, if it had been, you would have noticed it?'

'Well, I didn't. Why is it so important, anyway?'

Yes, why was it? Sarah felt that in some way which

6

she did not understand its disappearance was as significant as its appearance had been in the first place. In fact, it somehow made it more so. One thing was certain: she couldn't produce any reason sufficiently logical to satisfy Alec. She shook her head, knowing that her inability to do so would only irritate him further. She was right.

'Really, Sarah, you are making a fuss about nothing.'

'I am not making a fuss. I just don't understand what could have happened to it, that's all.'

She turned away from him, her eyes scanning the rest of the room, probing into shadowy corners, fruitlessly seeking the tell-tale flash of white which would betray its hiding place. Her gaze paused for a moment on the tableau reflected in the large mirror which hung between the two windows on the wall opposite the fireplace: Alec in profile, the fire and lamplight behind him outlining sharply the tall figure inclined impatiently towards her; herself turned away from him, repudiating his attitude, straight brown hair two dark smudges on either side of the pale blur that was her small, undistinguished face.

Alec was clearly taken aback at her reaction. It was unusual for Sarah to defend herself. 'All right, calm down.'

'I'm not uncalm.'

Alec gave an exasperated sigh. 'Well, I still can't see . . . oh, never mind, let's finish supper.'

Sarah allowed herself to be led back into the kitchen. The card was gone and that was that. Alec, obviously thinking that she was tired and overwrought, insisted on doing the washing-up and Sarah wandered back into the sitting-room. She sat down restlessly on the edge of the settee, looked speculatively at the place where the card should be and wondered why she felt that it was so important for her to know what had happened to it.

Perhaps . . . She rose and looked quickly around for a similar piece of card. There was an old birthday card in the drawer of her writing desk, if she remembered aright. Yes, there it was. The paper wasn't quite as thick, but it would do. Swiftly, guiltily, she hunted out a pair of scissors and cut out a piece of card as near to the dimensions of the other as possible. She could hear Alec moving about in the kitchen and could tell from the sounds that he had finished the washing-up and was making the coffee. She hadn't much time.

Pushing the mutilated birthday card and the pair of scissors back into the drawer, she went to the fireplace and carefully stood the card as near as possible to where she had put the other. She stood back. That was it. Now . . . very conscious of the heat of the fire burning into her distended stomach as she stretched up, Sarah delicately put out her little finger and edged the card off the beam, swinging herself clumsily around and away as it fell, so as not to impede its fall.

It fluttered to the ground and lay, white against the dark red patterned carpet, some two feet in front of the hearth. She picked it up, replaced it on the beam and repeated the experiment, this time blowing gently from the direction of the kitchen door. It had occurred to her that there might have been a draught from that direction when Alec went into the kitchen from the sitting-room after lighting the fire.

Nothing happened. She blew again, harder, and the card fluttered once more to the ground, just as Alec came in, carrying the coffee cups. It landed approximately the same distance away from the hearth, only slightly to the right, and Sarah bent as swiftly as she could to pick it up, hoping that Alec had not seen. Too late.

'Is that it, Sarah?'

'No, it's not.'

'Well, what is that card you are holding?'

8

'Nothing, really.'

'It can't be nothing. Let me see.'

'It's only a piece of card I cut out of an old birthday card.'

'Whatever for?'

'To see if I could find out if that other card might have fallen in the fire.'

Alec thumped the coffee cups down on to a nearby table so violently that the coffee slopped over into the saucers. 'Now look, Sarah, what sort of game are you playing?'

'Game?'

'Yes, game. Cutting up bits of card and experimenting with angles of fall and so on. I really would like to know why it is so important.'

'I don't know why. It just is.'

'Come here.' His exasperation showed not only in his voice but in the roughness of his grip on her wrist. Nevertheless, he was gentle as he pulled her towards the settee and lowered her on to it. He sat down beside her. 'All right, it's important to you, so let's work it out. You put the card on the beam. You are quite sure of that?'

Sarah nodded dumbly, miserably. She had known that Alec would be angry and her inattention at supper had only made things worse. Perhaps, though . . . She sat up straighter and tried to concentrate. She had heard Alec's logical mind at work often enough to know that if he brought it to bear on a problem he would usually manage to solve it.

'Right. So there it was, on the beam. And now it has gone. So there are two possibilities. Either it fell off by accident – in a draught, or because it wasn't properly balanced. Or someone took it off. You are quite sure you didn't move it yourself?'

Sarah shook her head. She couldn't speak. She knew suddenly, blindingly, why she had felt upset, uneasy.

9

Alec had led her in just a few words straight to her fear, until then unformulated. It was important to discover if the card had fallen into the fire because if it hadn't, then someone had taken it. And she knew *she* hadn't, so who could have done so?

'Well, you see how ridiculous any other possibility would be. Who on earth would wish to do such a thing?'

The person who put it in my bag in the first place, of course, screamed Sarah inwardly. But she couldn't tell Alec that; he would think that she was losing her mind. Alec took her silence for assent. 'So that's that then. Let's have our coffee and forget about it.' He took her face in his hands and tilted it gently up to his. 'There's nothing the matter, is there, darling? Nothing really the matter? You're feeling all right?'

'Yes, I'm fine. It's the waiting, I suppose, wondering if everything will be all right.'

'Of course it will. Why shouldn't it be? The doctor is quite satisfied, isn't he?'

Sarah nodded. Logic again. Couldn't Alec see that logic wasn't enough, that one could sometimes be afraid without apparent reason, feel something strongly and know instinctively that one is right to feel it, without being able to explain why?

His questions had reminded her of the panic which had swept over her that morning. She had gone up to the nursery to install her latest purchase for the baby – a tiny reclining chair in which he would be able to sit and watch the world about him. As she had carried it up the stairs she had imagined him in it, gurgling as he watched her moving about her work, but the moment she had entered the nursery the air of stillness in there had triggered off the terror again.

Sometimes the waiting was unbearable. She supposed that every pregnant woman had these terrifying thoughts, that her child might be still-born, handicapped, or even hideously deformed, a monster. She couldn't believe that they obsessed her more than most women, but more and more often lately the fear would descend upon her, consuming her in its intensity, leaving her weak and shaken. It did, after all, happen; every day there were women who gave birth to a lifetime of despair. It was hard, very hard not to be afraid, to reassure herself that of course it would be all right, all would go well, the baby would be perfect.

There had been many occasions lately when she had been on the verge of spilling it all out to Alec. It would be such a relief to talk it all out of her system. But she had an uneasy feeling that he would be inclined either to dismiss her fears as absurd or to try to reason them away, and so she always held back at the last moment. And certainly this was not the right time. Coming on top of the business of the card, Alec would think that she was becoming positively neurotic. Aware that he was awaiting some further reassurance from her, she took a deep, slow breath and managed a faint smile.

Alec's smile in response had the unmistakable stamp of relief. The crisis, thank God, was over, it said. Now we can return to normality. 'Come on, darling. Have some coffee and cheer up.' He went and fetched her coffee for her and Sarah obediently sipped the now lukewarm liquid. It was no good; she couldn't subjugate the fears by force of will. She might hold them in abeyance but the moment she relaxed they flooded back. If only I could be sure, she thought. If only, somehow, I could know that the baby will be all right. I couldn't bear it if anything went wrong now.

'It's a boy, Mrs Royd.'

'Is he . . . all right?'

'Now don't you worry about anything. Just go to sleep and rest yourself.'

'But the baby. Let me see him. I want to hold him.'

'Later, dear. You have a nice sleep now.'

And the fear of what she would see when she looked at the baby fused with the fear of the unknown hand dropping the card into her bag, the faceless figure reaching up to take it from the beam. Her cup rattled in her saucer and Alec was at her side.

'Sarah, are you sure you're all right?'

'Yes, of course.' Again she forced a smile in the direction of the tall, anxious figure stooping over her. Alec may be irritable, impatient, but his concern for her was genuine. She put out her hand and gripped his firmly, taking comfort from the physical contact, the reality of the bones beneath the flesh, the solidity of his presence. 'Let's see what's on television, shall we?'

But now, his anxiety aroused, Alec was not satisfied. 'Perhaps you ought to see Doctor Blunsdon tomorrow.'

Sarah shook her head. If she did, and told him what was the matter with her, he would put her on tranquillizers, and she didn't want that. She put as much conviction as she could muster into her voice. 'No, I'm fine, really, darling. I went to the clinic this morning, and everything is fine.' She really had been to the clinic, and everything really had been satisfactory, so she ended with a ring of truth which seemed to satisfy him.

But when the screen was lit up she sat in front of it, aware of the figures moving across it, aware of the companionable crackling of the log fire, aware of the glow cast by the standard lamp behind them, the warmth of Alec's arm about her shoulders, but totally separate from them all, conscious only of the fear, and of the small voice within her whispering over and over again, 'It will be all right, won't it? Oh God, please let it be all right. It will be, won't it?'

Chapter Two

'It's going to be another lovely day.'

Sarah nodded contentedly. They always lingered over breakfast on Saturdays, reading the newspapers and drinking second cups of coffee in a leisurely manner, relishing the fact that there was no rush for Alec to leave for work, that they could do as they wished in the hours that lay ahead.

She sat now, basking in the early-morning sunshine which always flooded the kitchen in fine weather, rocking gently in the cane rocking chair which Alec had found and brought home for her a few months before.

'Now you'll be able to rock away the hours until November,' he had said, planting it firmly down in the sunniest corner of the kitchen.

And Sarah loved it. She loved the delicate, intricate patterns of the basket-work, the companionable creaks and squeaks given forth by the expanding and contracting cane-work even when she was not sitting in it. At first they had startled her, but now they were merely the idiosyncrasies of an old friend.

She stopped rocking as Alec refilled both their coffee cups and handed hers to her. She sipped the strong fragrant liquid and gazed reflectively out of the window. The light mist which had lain in the orchards, wreathing the trunks of the apple trees, had lifted now and it was going to be another golden day. It had been one of the most beautiful autumns she could ever

13

remember – the long hot days had followed each other in endless succession and wherever one went people murmured incredulously about the weather, speculated upon when it would end, revelled in the unexpected benediction of warmth and sunshine so late in the year.

For Sarah it had seemed fitting that this autumn should be especially beautiful. She had always loved the autumn – all the really special things in her life seemed to have happened then. It was in the autumn that she had met Alec; in the autumn of the following year they had married, and it was in the autumn, too, that they had found the cottage. But this autumn held the rarest promise of them all, and putting down her cup, she folded her hands across the bulge which was so soon to become her child and sighed with satisfaction at the jerky, unco-ordinated movements she felt beneath them. It had been five long years before she had conceived and the thought that he was about to become real, visible, flesh and blood at last, was her last thought at night, her first thought in the morning.

She glanced up at the calendar, where twenty-three neat crosses already marked the page for October. Only twenty-seven more in all now, if her dates were right. In her mind's eye she saw the circle drawn around November 20th on the next page and again she visualized the moment when she would see her baby for the first time. This time, however, shaped by optimism, the scene was very different from the one her imagination had conjured up last night.

'It's a boy, Mrs Royd.' (Or a girl – what did it matter?)

'Is he . . . all right?'

'Of course, he's perfect. Look.'

And the exquisite sense of fulfilment as the baby was placed in her arms for the first time, the . . .

'You're looking very cheerful this morning.' Alec's voice broke into her thoughts.

'Yes, I'm fine.' She smiled at him, somewhat guiltily. Like the mists her fears of the night before had dispersed, leaving her wondering why it was she had been in such a state over such a trivial incident. She felt thoroughly ashamed of herself and was glad that she had not confided to Alec her fear that the whole thing had been deliberate.

She had lain awake for hours after they had gone to bed: first of all, struggling to fight off the panic which had still gripped her; then, when she had finally succeeded in calming herself, trying to work out why she had felt it.

In the end she had come to the conclusion that it had been the wording of the card that had triggered it off. In the first place it had further diminished the mood of joyful anticipation which had, until recently, been carrying her on over these difficult last few weeks before the baby came, and which had been undermined by those more and more frequent periods of panic like the two she had experienced yesterday; and then the words 'for thou knowest not what a day might bring forth' had tapped her perfectly natural fear of bearing a handicapped child.

Having reassured herself in this way, and decided that, if she had not been in this particularly vulnerable position, she would no doubt have torn the card up in the first place, she had been able to go to sleep. This morning, her equilibrium restored, she felt carefree and full once more of that dreamy happiness which had until a week or two ago been her constant companion through the last few months. Alec's suggestion, when it came, fitted in so well with her mood that she received it with delight.

'What about going out for the day? Perhaps we could take a picnic to the sea.'

'What a lovely idea! We haven't been to the sea for ages.'

Alec looked slightly smug. 'I thought it might do you good to have a breath of sea air. You had me worried last night. And there can't be many more days like this to come. This spell of fine weather has been going on for so long that, once it ends, winter will be upon us.'

'It's a wonderful idea. I'll make a picnic.'

By half past ten they were ready and drove out of their gate in a holiday mood. As they reached the end of the lane and turned left on to the main road they noticed a young boy in his early teens unloading apples from some boxes stacked nearby on to a rough trestle table which he had set up beside the road.

'Mr Turner is running true to form,' said Alec with a grin.

Sarah smiled back. 'I don't suppose he could bear not to.'

Mr Turner was their nearest neighbour, and a fruit farmer. The house in which Sarah and Alec lived had been his until 1971 when rocketing prices had tempted him into selling it. When the Royds moved in, he had bought a battered caravan, installed it in the farmyard adjoining their garden and run his farm from there. His short, wiry figure, dressed invariably in checked shirt, faded trousers and battered trilby, was a familiar sight in the orchards – and his meanness was a legend in the neighbourhood.

Anything he could sell, he would sell. The stall they had just passed was set up every year, and Mr Turner's nephew manned it, selling the windfalls which most fruit farmers did not bother to collect up. It was a tradition that the windfalls were a bonus, free to the women who did the seasonal work picking fruit in the orchards, but not on Mr Turner's farm. He had to employ pickers, he could not manage without them, but they would be paid as little as possible and certainly would not get any bonuses in the way of free windfalls if he could help it. Consequently pickers went to other fruit farmers for employment first, but Mr Turner always got his labour in the end because so many families relied upon the extra money which fruit picking brought in that they could not afford to boycott him if it meant being without work for a season.

Sarah smiled reminiscently. 'I still haven't forgotten when he picked our apples for us!' There had been a great deal of work to do that first autumn and Sarah had been delighted when Mr Turner had presented himself at the back door, turning his old trilby round and round in his hands. She had thought it most neighbourly of him to offer to pick their apples. She had not expected him to do it for nothing, of course, but neither had she expected him to sell the lot, without offering them either apples or a share in the proceeds. She had first been incredulous, then furious when she had found out. So had Alec, and it was with great difficulty that Sarah had restrained him from going round to Mr Turner's caravan and saying so in no uncertain terms.

'It won't do any good, Alec. There's no point. It'll only get us off to a bad start here.'

Alec had reluctantly agreed, and they had later found to their amusement that the incident had had the opposite effect. Victims of Mr Turner's meanness were legion, and they had found themselves immediately as one of the club. They had never discovered how other people had found out, but had assumed that the story must have been put about by one of his frustrated pickers. Mr Turner must have realized that he would not get away with it again, for he had never repeated his offer.

Now it was a joke between them and they exchanged smiling glances. Alec seemed to be in a very good mood, and Sarah wondered briefly if this would be a good moment to broach once again the subject of his being present at the birth of the baby.

This had been a bone of contention between them

for months. Sarah had assumed that he would want to be there, and had been bitterly disappointed when she had discovered that he was strongly opposed to the idea. They had argued about it from time to time ever since, and on the last occasion Alec had become very angry.

'For God's sake, leave it, Sarah!' he had shouted. 'I won't do it because I can't. I'm not that sort of person. It's too private, too intimate, too personal. Now forget it, will you?'

But she couldn't. Usually, if she and Alec disagreed about something, she would fall in with his wishes. Only occasionally, when it really mattered to her, as this did, would she persevere. Now, remembering how angry he had been last time, she reluctantly acknowledged that it seemed most unlikely that he would ever change his mind. In any case it would be a pity to spoil today with yet another argument about it. She settled back in her seat and prepared to enjoy herself.

And certainly, in the beauty all around them, there was much to enjoy. As if nature were hurrying to reach the peak of its autumn beauty before the weather broke, the reds, oranges and yellows of the autumn leaves were daily becoming more intense, and there were great swathes of colour flung across the countryside. The car wound its way along country lanes where the apricot of field maple, the dried-blood-red of dogwood, the golden gleam of oak and the white fluffiness of Old Man's Beard sped by them in a never-ending kaleidoscope of colour. Sarah and Alec murmured to each other from time to time, pointing out this or that of particular interest, but content on the whole to sit in silence and feast their eyes on the splendour before them.

It seemed strange, after this, to walk down on to the summer beach. The stretch of coastline which Alec had chosen was characterized by wide, open stretches of

18

shingle backed by dunes. When there was an on-shore wind the lack of shelter made it uninviting and uncomfortable but, wind or no, the summers always filled it with crowds of people determined to enjoy themselves. Now, today, with only a gentle off-shore breeze stirring the tufts of wiry grass on the sand-dunes, and the counter-attraction of the football season under way, Sarah and Alec had it almost to themselves. They picked a spot sheltered by a tall dune and settled down to enjoy the luxuries of sun, sea and solitude.

A motor cruiser skimmed across the surface of the bay, and Alec sat up to watch. 'I saw Frank yesterday, I forgot to tell you. He has a new car, a Jensen. What's the matter?'

Sarah, too, had struggled into a sitting position. 'I forgot to ask you. Have you got anything on next Wednesday? That's October 29th.'

'No, I don't think so. Why?'

'I had a letter from Angela yesterday, inviting us to dinner.'

'You don't sound very pleased about it.'

'I'm not. I suppose we'll have to go this time. She sounded a bit hurt, I thought. Let me see, I think I put the letter in my bag. Yes, here it is. See what you think.'

'A bit hurt? Let me see . . . yes . . . I see what you mean. "Mary and David are coming, so hope you can make it this time." Yes, she does sound a bit put out. It's not surprising, really. The last twice – or is it three times? – she's invited us, we've made some excuse. I can never understand why you don't want to go anyway. You like Angela, don't you?'

'Yes, of course I do.'

'Then why on earth are you always so reluctant to accept invitations from her? Is it Frank?'

'No, not really. He doesn't worry me.'

19

'You don't find it somewhat wearing to have him constantly making passes at you?'

Sarah laughed. 'Do I detect a hint of jealousy, darling?'

'Well, I must admit that I have had to restrain myself from punching him on the nose once or twice.'

'But you don't take him seriously, surely. Frank can't help flirting. It's in his nature, part of him, like his moustache.'

'No, I don't. If I did, I can assure you that we would have stopped going there long ago. But I still find it embarrassing, and I should think most husbands would. That's one of the reasons I think we ought to go.'

'I don't understand.'

'Well, I feel sorry for Angela. It must be embarrassing for her, having a husband who can't help playing up to all her women friends.'

'Sorry, for Angela?' Sarah was astounded.

'Yes, don't you?'

'Well, no, I'd never thought of it in quite that light. Now that you put it like that, of course, I can see what you mean.'

'Well, if you like Angela, as you say, and it isn't Frank's attentions which put you off, what does make you so reluctant to go there, then? I never have understood.'

'You won't laugh at me?'

'Of course not, why should I?'

'Promise?'

'Sarah, I said I wouldn't.' There was a hint of exasperation in his tone now.

'Oh, Alec, don't be cross. It's just that – ' and, seeing his face – 'well, Angela always . . . paralyses me.'

'What on earth do you mean?'

'Well, she is so perfect. She's so beautiful, always exquisitely dressed and immaculately groomed; and on top of that she is intelligent, kind, considerate, sincere, always ready to do anything for anybody. I do like her and I feel very guilty when I refuse her invitations because I'm sure she gets very hurt about it, but I can't help feeling as I do.'

'You make her sound too good to be true.'

'Well, that's how I see her. And she makes me feel dowdy, insignificant, uninteresting, a . . . nothing.'

There was silence. Eventually Alec stirred. 'Do you know how I see her?'

Sarah shook her head.

'I see her as a woman who can't afford not to be those things.'

'What do you mean?'

'Well, I think that, for all his womanizing, she really loves Frank. Now, put yourself in her position. She has so many potential rivals that the only possible way to defeat them is to be more everything than they are. More beautiful, better dressed, kinder, more understanding, everything. She has constantly to watch herself, be on her guard against relaxing these standards. Do you see what I mean?'

There was a further silence, longer this time. Sarah felt thoroughly ashamed of herself. Alec often made her feel like this. He seemed to have an insight into people which she was quite unable to attain. Perhaps it was because he was so much older than she was. Fifteen years was a big difference, after all. 'Alec, I'm sorry. Of course I see, now. Why ever didn't I see it before?'

'Because, my love, you were too preoccupied with your own feelings. You're far too introspective for your own good – and have far too low an opinion of yourself as well.'

'I can't help feeling inferior.' Sarah was slightly sulky now.

'You can't have much respect for my judgement, then.'

'Alec, you know that's not true.'

'Well, I chose you, didn't I?'

'I can't think why.'

She caught his eye and began to laugh. He joined in. Neither of them could have said what was so funny, but they both enjoyed it. Eventually Sarah wiped her eyes and said, 'I'll ring Angela when we get home, and tell her we'd love to come.' And there the matter was left.

It was half-past five when they reached home, drowsy and content after the hours of sea air and sunshine. The sun, a globe of incandescent crimson, was sinking slowly on to the western horizon, the bands of rosy light flung across the sky promising further fine weather to come. Sarah sighed with pleasure as the house came into view. She felt relaxed, secure, invulnerable and was looking forward to the pleasant evening ahead, curtains drawn against the swiftly approaching darkness, fire lit against the autumnal chill.

Alec dropped her by the front door and went on to lock the car away in the garage for the night. She stood for a moment, looking at the house, breathing in the scent of the few late crimson roses which hung motionless in the still air over the little front porch. 'Just look at the roses around the door,' Alec had said when he first told her about the house, 'and ignore the state of the inside.' But she hadn't needed to ignore anything; she had known as soon as she saw it that it was the house for them.

It stood now, neat and trim in its setting of lawns and flower-beds, very different from the neglected picture it had presented that autumn four years before. The blackness of the beams criss-crossing its walls, the crisp whiteness of the plaster between them and the fresh paint on door and windows all bore witness to the many hours of hard work which she and Alec had bestowed upon them.

With a familiar surge of proprietary pleasure Sarah unlocked the yellow front door and went inside. In contrast to the early evening coolness outside, the air in the hall was warm and stuffy with the pent-up heat of the day, and she left the door wide open. She felt sticky and grubby after the hours on the beach. She would have a quick shower before supper.

At the top of the stairs the open nursery door drew her like a magnet, as it so often did. She rarely passed it without pausing and glancing in and lately, since the work on it had been finished, she would often drift in and stand, as she did now, admiring her handiwork and anticipating the time when the room would come alive.

She had worked so hard in here. As soon as she had known that she was pregnant at last she had begun, and the room was now equipped to the last detail. No ordinary wallpaper for their baby – she had spent many hours painstakingly drawing and painting, and around the walls cut-out figures of Winnie the Pooh, Piglet, Eeyore and the rest waited to delight him.

On the white-painted chest of drawers sat three toys: two teddy bears and a doll. One of the bears was new, yellow and immaculate, the other bald and battered. It had been hers, and its appearance was a testimony to the love she had borne it. The doll was called Clementine and she, too, showed the marks of wear, but her painted china head and soft rag body had been Sarah's constant companion, and if the baby was a girl Sarah thought that perhaps she might enjoy Clementine's company too.

This room faced east and the light in here was fading fast, the bright colours becoming dimmer by the moment. Drawn by the square of brightness that was the window, Sarah drifted across to it, running her finger-tips caressingly along the handle of the pram, the side of the cot as she passed by. She stumbled over something on the floor and looked down, frowning.

She really must do something about this one incongruous note in the nursery: a pile of books and papers belonging to her father. Until the spring of this year the nursery had been a junk room and Sarah had gradually cleared it, either storing things elsewhere or throwing them away until only these remained. She had sorted out most of her father's possessions after his death four years ago, but she hadn't quite known what to do with these, and it would take some time to go through them properly.

She stopped now and picked up the book which lay on top of the pile: a handsome volume bound in green tooled leather. This was a scrapbook of her father's years as a judge, kept by her mother from the time he was made a judge until she died, three years before her husband.

Sarah stared blindly at the book in her hands, struggling to suppress the emotion it aroused in her. It was, for her, far more than just a scrapbook. It symbolized the relationship between her parents, the all-consuming interest which they had had in each other, so that there was nothing left for her.

How often, before she had been sent away to boarding school, had she come home from school, bursting with the day's events and found her mother with this book open on the table before her, busy with scissors and glue. The tips of Sarah's fingers turned white with the intensity of her grip on the leather as she felt the pain of those encounters clutch at her once more.

'Mummy, I had a star for my writing today. One of the tadpoles died and we – '

'Not now, Sarah, I'm busy. Tell me later. Come and say good night before you go to bed, you can tell me then. Run along and wash your hands. Janet has your tea ready.'

'But, Mummy – '

'Run along now. You can see I'm busy.'

And, even more agonizingly, her father's attitude to her had been the same. A detached, seemingly cold man, his emotions had never been deeply touched by a woman until, at the age of thirty-four, he met Sarah's mother, whose dark vivid beauty had at once captivated his heart, his mind and his imagination.

Some ten years younger than he and very much in demand socially, she had astounded him by declaring her intention of marrying nobody but himself, and a few months later they were married. Theirs had been a relationship profoundly satisfying to them both and by the time Sarah unexpectedly appeared on the scene some twelve years later there was, quite simply, no room for her in their full lives. Although neither of them was ever deliberately unkind to her, she had always felt superfluous, unimportant to them, an intruder in their ordered world and in the pleasure which they found in each other's company.

As she stood now, gazing sightlessly into the past, Sarah remembered one of the rare occasions when, her mother being out, her father had given her his undivided attention. She remembered the bliss of sitting on his lap and breathing in his special smell of tobacco, shaving lotion and clean linen and how she had felt when her mother had come in, cheeks flushed from the frosty air outside, eyes shining beneath her small fur hat. And how she, Sarah, had at once quite simply ceased to exist for him as he put her aside and went to take her mother's outstretched hands.

She slammed the scrapbook down on top of the pile and turned away. She couldn't bear to burn it, yet she still couldn't bear to read it. Outside, the washing-line and the kitchen garden immediately below were in shadow, and so was part of the line of fast-growing Cupressus trees which they had planted in their first autumn here to define their boundary and to shut out the jumble of dilapidated buildings beyond. The young trees were about five feet tall now and already screened the ugly buildings from the kitchen. By the time the baby was old enough to notice views, they would no doubt have grown to a living green wall, twenty or more feet high.

From where she stood, Sarah could just see the door of Mr Turner's caravan over to the right behind the low stone building which they had bought with the house and turned into a garage, but the farmyard was deserted and Sarah was about to turn away from the window when her attention was caught by a tiny flash of light. Puzzled, she turned back again. Where had it come from? There it was again, over to the left in the orchard. What could it be? There were no windows or glass of any kind over there to reflect the sun. Perhaps one of the pickers had discarded a lemonade bottle or something similar. But it couldn't be that. If it were, the reflection of light would be constant.

Suddenly she was back on a sunny hillside in Wales. They had lain down on a couch of bracken, and Alec had just taken her in his arms when he had pushed her fiercely away and jumped to his feet. 'Damned peeping Tom. Look.' His finger, thrust out accusingly, had pointed out the place and Sarah had seen it come and go, a tiny pin-point of light far above them on the slope.

As if to confirm her memory the tiny spot of light flashed again in the orchard. There was no room for doubt. Someone was watching the house through binoculars.

Chapter Three

Automatically she wheeled around, so that her back was against the curtain and she was hidden from view. She must be wrong, surely. She must be. What possible interest could anyone have in watching their house? Her fears of the night before came flooding back, redoubled in intensity. She must call Alec. He must see for himself, then he would believe her.

She risked another peep, waited a few moments until the flash came again, then tip-toed to the top of the stairs and waited. She could hear Alec outside on the drive, walking towards the open front door, and as soon as he appeared she whispered loudly, 'Alec.'

He looked up, the surprise on his face intensifying as he saw her standing at the top of the stairs, finger to her lips. 'Sarah? Whatever is the matter?'

'Shh. Come up here.'

He began to climb the stairs. 'What on earth are you whispering for?'

As he reached the top she took him by the arm and drew him into the nursery. She guided him, puzzled and uncomprehending, to stand behind one of the curtains, then, pointing, said, 'Look out there.'

He looked, obediently, and Sarah waited expectantly for his exclamation of anger. 'Well? I've looked. Now what?'

'Can't you see him?'

'See whom?'

'The man watching the house.'

Alec took one more incredulous look out of the window and turned to Sarah. 'What are you talking about?'

'When I looked out of the window a few moments ago there was a man watching the house through binoculars.'

'Well, there isn't now. Look for yourself.'

And there wasn't. He waited until she was satisfied, then led her firmly downstairs into the kitchen. He sat her down in the rocking chair and looked at her gravely for a few moments in silence. Finally he said, 'You really believe this, Sarah?'

'Well, I saw it, quite clearly.'

'You actually saw the man, watching the house?'

'Not exactly. I saw the light reflected off his binoculars.'

'You don't think it possible that what you saw might have been the sunlight reflected off a piece of broken glass?'

'I did think of that, but it couldn't have been, because then it would have been constant.'

'Not if you had moved even fractionally. In that case you would have moved out of the line of the angle of reflection.'

Sarah conceded that this could be so. 'In that case, why didn't you see it?'

'Because the sun is sinking so fast by now that something might well have come between the sun and it – a branch, a twig, a leaf.'

'I suppose you're right.'

'Don't be so grudging about it. Anyone would think you would prefer it to be someone watching the house rather than accept the logical explanation.'

'Don't be silly, Alec.' Logic again, she thought resentfully.

'Well, that is certainly the impression you give.' He

turned away with a gesture of impatience. 'I don't know what is the matter with you these days. First, there was that business with the card last night, now this. And you seem to disagree with everything I say.'

Sarah sat, silent. What could she say? It was all true.

Abruptly his mood changed and, coming across to her, he took her hands. 'Look, love, don't you think that perhaps you are letting your imagination run away with you? After all, what possible reason could there be for anyone to watch the house?'

'I know that.' But she was unconvinced. She remembered the feeling of absolute certainty with which she had known that there was someone with binoculars out there, watching, and the fear clutched at her again. Suddenly she felt the tears rising and she buried her head in her hands, abandoning herself thankfully to them.

Alec crouched down before her, put his arms around her and stroked her hair wordlessly.

As she leaned gratefully against him and enjoyed the luxury of tears, Sarah felt like a stone within her the knowledge that this was only a temporary release and solved nothing, that something, somewhere, was radically wrong. But what?

Alec waited until she was relatively calm again, then tilted her chin up towards him with his forefinger. 'Better?'

She nodded.

'You know, I think perhaps the real trouble is that you are worrying abut the baby. Try not to, darling. I know this is a bad time, with nothing to do but wait, but there really is no reason to be afraid, is there?'

But I don't even know what I am afraid of any more, thought Sarah dully. Everything is becoming so confused and the fears are overlapping and merging.

'Why don't you have a long, hot bath? I'll see to things down here. It might help you to relax.'

She allowed herself to be persuaded up the stairs and into the bedroom. Alec ran the bath while she slowly undressed, her mind a blank. But in the bath, with the mound of her distended stomach rising before her a perpetual reminder of her condition, the worries came rushing back.

Was she imagining it all? She hadn't imagined the card, that was certain. She could see it still, the printed black capitals stark against the white background. But the rest of it, the dread that it might have some sinister significance (but what?), the fear that someone might have deliberately removed it (but why and when?), the conviction that there had been someone watching the house (but for what possible reason?), was all that in her mind the figment of a disordered imagination?

She had always been inclined to imagine the worst, to conjure up scenes of disaster, but she had always been aware that they were fantasies. This was different; this was too close to reality for comfort. Was it simply that she was in a hyper-sensitive state at the moment, the tension which had been building up in her for weeks now making her more liable to be thrown off balance easily, to lose her sense of proportion more quickly? Alec obviously thought so, and usually she trusted his judgement implicitly.

It was, she conceded, much more likely that he should be right than that she should. Ordinary people, such as Alec and herself, did not receive threatening messages on disappearing cards, were not watched by anonymous figures with binoculars, did not plunge from a pleasant, ordinary, mundane existence into melodrama for no apparent reason. And she had, understandably, been on edge lately. Perhaps she was reading too much into perfectly ordinary events – a card dropped into a handbag by some religious crank and subsequently blown into the fire by a draught; the glint of sunlight off a piece of broken glass carelessly dropped by an apple picker. From now on she would make a determined effort to be sensible.

She took some care over dressing, choosing one of the dresses Alec liked best, high-necked and long-sleeved in a heavy linen the colour of fallen leaves. His appreciative smile when she came downstairs lifted her spirits and strengthened her resolution.

It was not until later, much later, when they were in bed and Alec's even breathing told her that he was asleep, that the suspicions began insidiously to creep back into her mind. Failing dismally to shut them out, she felt rising within her, as inexorably as the tide, the panic which had kept her awake for so long the night before and in desperation she sat up, as if physical movement would suppress it. She couldn't face another night like last night. The memory of the long hours through which she had lain awake, staring into the darkness, made her press clenched hands to her temples as if to blot it out. Anything would be preferable to repeating that experience. She would take a sleeping pill.

Taking care not to wake Alec, she put aside the bedclothes and padded to the bathroom. A few minutes' search in the medicine cabinet produced the sleeping pills, which had been prescribed for her early on in her pregnancy but had never been used. She hated taking drugs of any sort and had studiously avoided doing so over the last months, for fear of any harm they might do to the baby. Doctor Blunsdon had assured her that it was quite safe to take these but she still felt guilty as she shook one out into the palm of her hand and ran some water into a tooth-glass. She hesitated for a moment longer, then, feeling as though she was conceding something, though she did not know what or to whom, she swallowed it down.

31

Chapter Four

The sunlight slanted in golden bars through the arched windows and haloed the heads of the choir boys. Dazzled, as they always were on sunny Sunday mornings, they sang heroically on, screwing up their eyes against the light, unconsciously shifting their heads from side to side in ineffectual attempts to evade it.

Sarah sang, too, hardly conscious of the meaning of the words which escaped her lips, aware only of the strength rising, like sap, within her. She had needed this, the sense of continuity and permanence which eased away that frightening sensation that foundations were crumbling beneath her feet. She had needed, too, the reassurance, implicit in the atmosphere of this tiny, ancient church, that in any struggle between the two, good would prevail over evil. Fleetingly she felt again the regret that Alec would never accompany her to church. His presence beside her would have reassured her still further.

The walk to church had shaken off the sluggish, depressed feeling with which she had awoken this morning – the after-effect, no doubt, of the sleeping pill. As her feet had scuffed up the fallen leaves, which lay like two brown ribbons along each side of the lane, she had taken in deep breaths of the clear, fresh air and vowed that, come what may, she would take no more pills.

The final, long-drawn-out 'Amen' roused her,

blinking, from her reverie, and she followed the other members of the sparse congregation through the ritual hand-shake with the Vicar at the door of the church.

On the way home she had almost reached the corner where she turned off the main road when she was startled by a long, gleaming white car which pulled up beside her.

'Hullo, Sarah. Long time no see. How are you?'

'Angela, Frank. Fine, thanks. What a beautiful car! How long have you had it?'

'Two days.' Frank sent her his usual self-consciously charming smile, eyes crinkling at the corner. 'Just showing Angie her paces, haven't had a chance before.'

'Alec was telling me about it yesterday. He said he'd seen you in town.' She stood awkwardly shifting her weight from one foot to the other. She felt hot and dusty in comparison with Angela who, as usual, was exquisitely groomed and dazzling in scarlet and white. Obviously she had dressed to complement the white body-work and leather seats of the new car. She also felt guilty at not having rung Angela before. She had intended to do so last evening, but the business of the man in the orchard had put it quite out of her mind. 'I got your letter, by the way. I was going to ring you later. We'd love to come.'

Angela, who had opened her mouth as if to speak, closed it again and smiled delightedly. Frank spoke for her. 'Good-oh. Look forward to seeing you then.' Another gleaming smile from him, a wave of Angela's arm and with a low-throated roar and a spurt of dust they were gone.

It wasn't until they were out of sight that Sarah realized that Angela had not spoken a single word during the whole of this encounter. Remembering what Alec had said on the beach, she went thoughtfully on her way. It had certainly made her reassess her ideas about Angela. If he was right, and she felt that he was,

33

Angela was in a most unenviable position. Always to live on a knife-edge of uncertainty, always to have to strive for something which she should surely to some extent be able to take for granted, always to see every other woman as a potential rival, must surely be an experience to eat away at one's self-esteem and lead eventually to despair. Yet she had never seen the slightest hint of this in Angela's behaviour.

Sarah's feet crunched down in anger upon the dried leaves beneath them as she thought about the bruised feelings Angela must nurse beneath that calm and elegant exterior. It wasn't even as though Frank were worth it. Sarah had never understood why Angela, who could have chosen from dozens of suitors, had married him. He was handsome, certainly, if one liked that kind of stereotyped good looks, all crinkly hair, flashing teeth and charm, but Sarah had yet to detect any admirable traits in his character. He was generous, she supposed. Angela always seemed to have plenty of money to spare and must spend a small fortune on clothes. Though perhaps even that was conscience money, she thought vindictively, and was immediately ashamed of herself.

All the same, she felt that her attitude to them both would be very different from now on. She would make it up to Angela somehow for her neglect and coldness in the past. Why, why hadn't she seen it all before? Alec was probably right. She had been far too concerned with her own feelings to spare a thought for Angela's. She was far too introspective for her own good. No doubt that, together with her unruly imagination, was the cause of all the trouble over the last few days.

The resolution to be more rational, less self-absorbed, more outward-looking carried her through the day and she went to bed reassured that tonight she would have no difficulty in sleeping. It was, therefore, all the more infuriating to find that, long after Alec had fallen asleep, she was still lying awake, staring into the darkness. It was always difficult to get to sleep these days, of course. For one thing, she always seemed to get heartburn at night. She had been assured that this would cease when the baby was born. Meanwhile it was not really painful, just extremely uncomfortable and not conducive to sleep. And then there was the fact that, however quiet the baby had been during the evening, when she got into bed and lay down he inevitably woke up and started kicking vigorously. Perhaps, she reflected as she had so often before, he was simply readjusting himself to the change of position. Normally she didn't mind, was in fact delighted: it was reassuring when he did that.

But tonight was different. She was very conscious of the fact that the previous evening she had had to take a sleeping pill, and very determined that it wasn't going to happen again. Unfortunately the determination itself seemed to be a barrier against the longed-for drowsiness. And then, too, deep down in her mind, trampled on and held down by force of will, was the memory of the reasons why she had had to take the pill. She was not going to let them come to the surface and disturb her again, and the conscious effort she had to make to prevent them from doing so also held sleep at bay.

Eventually she gave up in despair. She still wouldn't take a pill, but she would get up and walk around a little. She went to the bathroom, then crossed the room to peer at the clock. One o'clock. She groaned inwardly at the prospect of all the hours ahead before daylight came. Perhaps some fresh air might help.

They had left the window at the front open, overlooking the drive, but she wanted to lean out and breathe in the scent of the garden, so she went across to the west casement and put up her hand to open it. As she did so, she froze. Surely there was someone standing at the far side of the lawn, a darker patch where there

35

ought to be none? Involuntarily she closed her eyes and when she opened them, it was gone. She was instantly furious with herself. If only she had left them open she would have known whether or not she had imagined it, she would have seen whether or not there had been any movement out there.

She opened the window with fingers clumsy with haste and leaned out as far as she comfortably could. Nothing stirred. There was no wind and no moon, and the shadows on the far side of the lawn were in any case not clearly defined, merely darker patches against a dark background. It must have been a trick of the light.

Closing her eyes she willed herself back into the calm she had found in church that morning. Her over-active imagination was not going to drag her away from the peace she had so newly won and plunge her once more into the misery of last night and the night before.

She waited until she was fairly sure of herself, then opened her eyes and looked again. Nothing. She shivered and became aware that the cold was seeping into her flesh under the nylon nightdress. She must get back to bed at once. If only she could sleep! She felt as alert as ever, perhaps more so. Glancing once more into the still innocent garden, she closed the window and, resigning herself to further hours of wakefulness, went back to bed.

But the warm haven that was the bed, the comfortable glow emanating from Alec as he slept, the sheer contrast with the chill she had felt at the window, combined to bring her to drowsiness, and at last, against all expectation, she slept.

Chapter Five

Sarah surfaced, tossing wet hair out of her eyes. Apart from herself the swimming pool was deserted, as it always was at this time in the morning. Years before she had seen a photograph of a pregnant woman undergoing some special treatment. She had been encased from neck to knee in some kind of inflated balloon. The effect, visually, was grotesque, but it was claimed that the children of women who had regularly had this treatment were far more intelligent and gifted than most. The principle, as far as Sarah understood it, was that during the sessions the baby in the womb was freed from any kind of pressure or pull of gravity and benefited from it enormously.

When she had become pregnant she had made enquiries about the possibility of having the treatment herself, but had been unable to find anyone who knew anything about it. She had reasoned that the nearest she would be able to come to such conditions would be while swimming, so very early on in her pregnancy she had formed the habit of going to a nearby pool twice a week.

She had found that from 8.30 until 9.45, when the first school parties arrived, the pool was, during term-time, deserted. During the holidays it was more difficult. As her body swelled she had often, during July and August, been forced to return home without having entered the water. She would have been too embarrassed to expose her pregnant self to the curious gaze of teenagers.

This morning she revelled in the freedom, the ease of movement, the sense of lightness which she always experienced in the pool. She felt that, even if the baby had not benefited directly, she certainly had. Swimming had been the only thing she had ever done well, and she hadn't realized how much she had missed it until she took it up again.

Now she glanced up at the clock on the wall and reluctantly decided that it was time to get out of the water. The attendant of this huge, heated indoor pool, Mr Rogers, was as usual keeping tactfully out of the way. He had been most helpful and encouraging all the way along and had developed, in the last two months, the knack of disappearing at times when he felt his presence might embarrass her. He had even, on one occasion, held back a school party which had arrived early, so that Sarah could remove herself to the changing rooms in privacy. She didn't want that to happen again, and she struck out for the metal ladder with a clean, powerful breaststroke, the sensation of clumsiness washing through her as she emerged from the water.

On the way home she stopped at the garage in the village for some petrol. Bill Mudge ran it alone, with the help of one apprentice. Tall and thin, with a thatch of unruly black hair and a pair of piercing blue eyes, he loved engines and would even talk to them coaxingly as he worked. He had steadfastly refused to go into the profitable, second-hand car side of the motor trade as it would have involved too much dashing about and giving time and attention to cars he would never see again. This morning he was bending lovingly over the engine of a battered old Austin as Sarah drew up.

'Morning, Bill. Two, please.'

'Morning, Mrs Royd. Keeping well, are you?'

'Fine, thank you. I'm still getting that rattle, occasionally.' They both knew what she meant.

Bill frowned. Unidentified rattles irritated him, and this one always disappeared the moment he laid hands on her car. 'If it gets worse, let me know.'

Sarah nodded agreement. 'I will.'

At home she left her swimming things on the bonnet of the car while she wandered around the garden. She felt restless, disinclined to settle down to doing the washing. She sniffed at the late roses, admired the brilliant scarlet of the Japanese Maple they had put in the previous autumn, and generally procrastinated. Eventually she found herself back at the car, having completed a circuit of the entire garden, and she decided that it was time she went in and got down to work.

First of all, though, she would hang up her wet bathing things. She took the rolled-up towel off the car bonnet and went across to the washing-line. She unrolled it carefully, so as not to drop her bathing costume on the ground, and as she did so, a small white card fell from its folds and fluttered to the ground.

She stared at it incredulously. Surely it couldn't be? She bent to pick it up, then hesitated. What if it wasn't the same card, but another one? The world narrowed to the slip of white pasteboard lying on the dusty path before her. It seemed to swell and diminish before her eyes. There was only one way to find out and slowly, reluctantly, she put out her hand and took it between her fingers.

Her throat was dry and she swallowed convulsively as she straightened up, holding the card away from her as if its very proximity had power to harm her. Then she turned it over. The words struck up at her like a physical blow, square printed capitals again, black and menacing:

TO EVERYTHING THERE IS A SEASON,
AND A TIME TO EVERY PURPOSE UNDER
THE HEAVEN. A TIME TO BE BORN, AND
A TIME TO DIE.

ECCLES. 111.1.

Where could it have come from? It certainly hadn't
been there when she left the swimming baths. The only
time the rolled-up towel had been left unattended was
while she had been walking around the garden. The
implication struck home and she cast a terrified glance
about her. She felt suddenly exposed, defenceless.
Hardly realizing what she was doing, she ran blindly
to the back door. It was locked, of course, and she
hurried around to the front, fumbling her key out of
her handbag as she went.

Shutting the door behind her, she leant against it for
a moment, regaining her breath, then went slowly into
the kitchen. Crossing to the table, she put the card
gently down on to the scrubbed wood and stood looking
at it.

If it had been slipped into her towel while she was
looking at the garden, then it had been done deliberately to frighten her. She could not this time delude
herself into thinking that she was one of many people
to receive one. The first time it had just been possible
to believe this, even though her instincts had rejected
the idea, but this time the spurt of venom was clearly
directed at her, and her alone.

Another terrifying aspect of the incident was that
someone was obviously keeping a very close watch on
her movements, to have been able to snatch at the
opportunity to push the card into her towel during the
short time it had been left unattended on the bonnet
of the car. How long had she been wandering around
the garden? Fifteen minutes, perhaps twenty? But she
had been in sight of the car much of the time, so the

period during which it could have been planted could not have been much longer than, say, ten minutes.

She felt cold, very cold, and folded her arms across her chest, hugging herself for comfort. Who could wish to do such a thing, and why? Whichever way she looked at it, it seemed quite incomprehensible, and this she found the most frightening aspect of all.

Perhaps – and she looked uneasily towards the window – he might still be out there, watching for her. She hurried upstairs and moved methodically from room to room, looking out of each window in turn. The difficulty was that, as she and Alec had often remarked, it was a splendid garden in which to play hide and seek. There were a number of large shrubs to provide dense cover, and Alec had surrounded the lawn with a pergola over which Sarah had trained climbing plants. Beyond this was rough grass and a number of old fruit trees. It would be easy to move from one part of the garden to another without being seen, provided one took care.

What should she do now? Ring Alec? He hated being rung at work, and she could imagine how he would react. She would ring Mary, perhaps go to see her. She had arranged to have coffee with her tomorrow; perhaps she could go today instead. The prospect of finding comfort in Mary's reassuring presence calmed her and she hurried downstairs to the sitting-room, dialled the number and waited eagerly, pressing the receiver impatiently to her ear. The dialling tone repeated itself monotonously and in sudden disappointment she realized that Mary must be out at work. Both Mary and David Godwin were teachers. After they were married Mary had continued teaching until their daughter was born. Lucy was now an engaging mopheaded urchin of five, and when she had started school in September, Mary had taken a part-time teaching post. Monday must be one of the mornings when she was out.

Sarah replaced the receiver and stood gazing abstractedly down at it. Should she ring Alec after all? Indecision gave way to anger. Why should she be driven out of her own home by this mysterious intruder into her life? Whoever he was, she would show him that he could not frighten her as easily as he might have thought. It was probably as well that Mary was out. How he would have loved to see her scurry off like a frightened mouse! Unconsciously she straightened her shoulders. She would carry on as usual. It was Monday, and washing day. Washing day it would be.

With grim determination she marched upstairs into the bathroom, emptied out the contents of the linen basket and began, doggedly, to sort them into their various piles: whites, coloureds, hand-washing. As the three piles grew and her body automatically became caught up in the momentum of the familiar washing-day routine, the anger and fear gradually seeped away, leaving bewilderment and uneasiness behind them.

After lunch she sat looking at the card, which still lay on the table where she had put it when she came in. Then she rose and fetched a heavy glass ashtray which she placed squarely upon it. This time it would not blow away or otherwise disappear. It would be there to show Alec when he came home. She had not mentioned to him the shadow she thought she had seen on the lawn last night. She had not been sufficiently sure about it and had in any case not wished to provoke another argument.

Now, she felt sure that there had been someone watching out there, and that the card before her was proof of it. Here, at last, was something tangible which would surely convince Alec that she had not been imagining it all. Now he would be able to see for himself, and everything would be all right. They would be able to talk about it sensibly, without him getting angry, and discuss what to do about it.

She picked up her cup and saucer and went over to the sink to wash them up. The kitchen was below the nursery and this window had a rather uninspiring view of the washing-line, with the line of young Cupressus trees beyond. Sarah looked with satisfaction at the result of her morning's labours moving idly on the line in the gentle breeze which had sprung up. There was still not enough wind to rotate the line but the sun was sufficiently hot for the clothes to be drying nicely. As she looked the breeze playfully lifted the corner of a sheet, held it suspended for a second, then dropped it again. Sarah gasped, involuntarily, the grip of her fingers tightening on the edge of the sink. She was quite sure that in that brief moment when the sheet had been upheld she had seen, framed between the tips of two Cupressus trees, a face.

Clearly, it was watching the house. She waited, breath held, for the sheet to lift again, but tantalizingly it would not rise quite far enough. Suddenly she was tired of all this wondering, waiting, watching. She would go out and challenge him. Without stopping to consider, she flung open the kitchen door, ducked under the washing and made straight for the place where she had seen it.

As she expected, it was gone, but she hurried on undeterred until she reached the trees, which were as tall as she was and thick and bushy at the base. Thrusting aside the foliage she leant forward, so that her head was projecting over the low fence beyond them into Mr Turner's yard. Surely she had been quick enough to catch him, or at least to glimpse him?

In front of her was an open space. Across the other side of it were the low, open-fronted sheds in which Mr Turner's pickers worked in the late afternoon, boxing up the apples gathered during the day. It was deserted. There was never anyone there at this time.

Immediately to her right was Mr Turner's decrepit

caravan, with a gap some four feet wide running between it and the back wall of Sarah and Alec's garage, which marked the boundary at that point. To her left was a large shed and between it and their Cupressus hedge was a narrow gap some two feet wide, quite wide enough, thought Sarah with sinking heart, for someone to squeeze through. One thing was certain. Whoever it was had gone. Much of the farmyard was hidden from where she stood and appeared in any case to be quite empty.

As if to prove her wrong, Mr Turner suddenly appeared from around the corner of the shed on her left, walking towards his caravan. There was no time for Sarah to withdraw and she forced an embarrassed smile as Mr Turner, astounded by the spectacle of her disembodied head poised between the tips of the evergreens, stopped abruptly in his tracks.

Sarah decided that no platitudes about the weather would serve. Nevertheless, she found difficulty in deciding how to put it. 'Oh . . . Mr Turner . . . I thought . . . I wondered . . . have you by any chance seen anyone lurking about in your yard?'

Mr Turner's eyes went immediately to the door of his caravan. He was apparently reassured by the sight of the large padlock hanging secure and untampered-with at the door. 'No, I haven't, Mrs Royd. Why would you be asking?'

'Well, I was looking out of the kitchen window just now and I thought I saw someone peering over into our garden. So I came to see.'

'No, I haven't seen nobody. Though I haven't been here, mind, not the last half hour or so, at any rate.'

'Well, if you do see anyone, perhaps you would let us know?'

'I will that. I don't want no strangers lurking about my property.' He turned away and walked purposefully up the two steps to the caravan door. Sarah, dismissed, disengaged herself from the hedge, feeling thoroughly foolish. Abstractedly she began unpegging clothes from the line, dropping the pegs into the peg-bag which hung from the tip of one of the arms of the rotary drier and draping the clothes roughly over her left arm. What should she do, what could she do now? She felt helpless, impotent. Whoever was watching her was clearly alert and quick off the mark, and she in her present state clumsy and slow.

She began to walk slowly back along the path to the kitchen door, turning the problem this way and that in her mind, arms piled high with fragrant clothes. She could not remember, later, what it was that made her glance to the left just before she reached the house. No doubt her mind, despite her preoccupation, subconsciously noticed that something was amiss, something was not as it should be.

The garage was a long stone building, originally one of the complex of buildings which formed the farmyard. At the far end, the end nearest the road, was a small lean-to shed, sturdily built of the same stone, in which Alec kept the lawn mower and tools for gardening and carpentry. He had had a stout lock fixed to the door after a series of burglaries in the neighbourhood a year or two back, and the shed was usually kept locked unless he or Sarah was using the tools.

Sarah was therefore surprised to see that the door of this shed stood slightly ajar, and immediately on the heels of surprise came fear. Surely it hadn't been open when she came home from swimming? And she hadn't noticed it on her many trips to and from the washing-line, either. Could the unknown watcher be in there now, relying on her curiosity to bring her to investigate and deliver her right into his hands?

Her mind leapt ahead, visualizing herself stepping into the darkness of the shed, the black shape leaping at her . . . She blinked, cutting off the sequence. Even in her worst imaginings she stopped short of actual violence. Violence was outside her experience, something which happened only to other people. She could not seriously believe that this person intended to cause her physical harm. She had, after all, been alone in the house most of the morning and he had done nothing. She was sure by now that his intention was to make her afraid, to confuse and torment her so that she would not know from which direction the next blow might fall.

She stood, hesitating. Terrifying though the thought of going to investigate might be, in one way it would bring relief. To see him face to face would be better than chasing shadows. An enemy with a face would be better than an enemy shaped by fantasy.

Still clutching the bundle of washing, which she obscurely felt gave her some protection, she started to move as quietly as possible towards the shed. It was only about twenty paces but it seemed an age before she reached it. The door, which opened outwards, stood only slightly ajar and there was complete silence from within. When she was close enough Sarah stood for a moment gathering courage, then reached out and swung it open. It crashed back against the wall on the far side and rebounded, quivering. The gap, however, was wider than before and daylight flooded the dark interior.

Cautiously Sarah peered around the door jamb. There was still no sound from inside, and she could see no movement. Encouraged, she advanced her head a little further. Her eyes, adapting themselves to the dimmer light in the further recesses of the shed, still picked up nothing out of the ordinary and after waiting a moment or two longer she finally took one step, then another into the little building.

She stood for a moment until she was sure that there was no one there. There was nothing sufficiently large for anyone to hide behind and, deflated, she turned to go outside again. As she did so she caught a flicker of movement out of the corner of her eye, and the door swung home with a click.

There was no window in the shed and Sarah stood in the pitch darkness, fighting the rising panic within her. Then, suddenly, she relaxed and almost laughed aloud with relief. She was not really shut in at all. The lock was of the Yale type, and she could walk out whenever she chose. All the same, she would wait a few minutes to get over her fright. Having now twice screwed up sufficient courage to face whoever it was who was playing these tricks, and twice having been disappointed, she felt quite unable to fling open the door and make another attempt at confrontation. For she was sure it had been no accident. The door had not swung shut of its own accord: someone had pushed it.

And she was not in the least surprised, when she got back to the kitchen, to find that the ashtray was still on the table, but that the card had gone from beneath it.

Chapter Six

It was not until shortly before Alec was due home from work that Sarah had her inspiration. She was still feeling relatively calm. Frightening and incomprehensible though the occurrences of the morning had been, they had at least given her some measure of reassurance that whoever was playing these tricks did not intend to hurt her physically. There had been plenty of opportunities to do that, and he had not taken them. After the episode in the shed she had decided that, if this was going to be a war of nerves, then she was going to win it.

She soon found, however, that it was easier to make this resolution than it was to keep it, and she spent the rest of the afternoon turning the matter over in her mind, trying to make sense of it. Why, why should anyone wish to frighten her? What possible reason, what possible motive could anyone have for behaving in this way? It was alarming indeed to think that she could have aroused this degree of animosity in anybody without being aware that she had done so. Could she really be as insensitive as that?

It was the cards which distressed her most of all. How right she had been to fear the first! She had known as soon as she saw it that it had had some personal significance for her. Whoever this person was, he had some insight into Sarah's mind and the fears that lurked there. Friday's card had been bad enough, but

48

this one was worse. 'A time to be born and a time to die.' The words repeated themselves over and over again in her mind, causing her to hug her arms protectively across her swollen belly in an agony of maternal love. Nothing, absolutely nothing, would harm her baby, if anything she could do would prevent it.

And she hated, too, the sense of being watched. When she went up to change, before starting to prepare supper, she even drew the curtains in the bedroom, so strong was her feeling that somewhere the unseen observer was lurking, aware of her every move. Before going downstairs she felt impelled, against her will, to look out of the window once more, to see if she could catch a glimpse of the watcher.

The sun had sunk below the horizon, but the sky to the west was still coral and rose, gold and amber, merging overhead into a soft luminous grey. On the far side of the lawn the late dahlias and chrysanthemums stood motionless in the still air, their colours muted in the fading light. There was no sign of the intruder, no flicker of movement to betray his hiding place, no indication whatsoever that all was not as it should be. If only it were as innocent as it looked! Sarah sighed, let the curtain fall and went downstairs to prepare supper.

She was peeling potatoes when the sound of Mr Turner's lorry starting up gave her the idea. The noise recalled him to her mind, together with the embarrassment she had felt when he had caught her peering over the hedge. The story would amuse Alec. It was reassuring to think that she now had someone else keeping an eye open for her persecutor. Two pairs of eyes were better than one, and when it came to protecting his property Sarah was sure that Mr Turner's eyes would be sharp indeed. Unless . . . her hands suddenly became still. What if Mr Turner himself was the man who was trying to frighten her?

The more she thought about it the more feasible it seemed. Certainly he was in a better position to keep a close watch on her than anyone else. He was always on the spot, always with a good reason for being so. He would have had as much opportunity as anyone else to slip the first card into her handbag on Friday while she was shopping. And no doubt this morning it would have been simple enough for him to put the second into her towel, to have been the face she saw behind the Cupressus hedge, to have slipped around to the workshed while she was taking down the washing, instead of going into his caravan. There would have been time. And his apparent astonishment at seeing her, his apparent concern that the padlock on his caravan should not have been tampered with, would all have been deliberate, calculated to put her off the scent.

The only difficulty was that she still couldn't see any possible reason for his wishing to frighten her. But the same was true of anyone else, and somehow Mr Turner, the familiar, was less frightening than a faceless stranger, whose menace was unfathomable.

She was so absorbed that she did not realize that Alec was home until the front door slammed. She swiftly decided that she would not mention any of this to him until after supper. Fortunately she was sufficiently in control of herself to be able to greet him as if nothing out of the ordinary had happened, but an unmistakable air of relief in his response made her realize that a difficult time lay ahead.

It was therefore with some diffidence that she eventually broached the subject. They were sitting by the fire drinking coffee. Sarah felt reluctant to spoil the relaxed and peaceful atmosphere, but knew she must. There could be no real peace until they reached some understanding on this matter, so she took a deep breath and began.

'Alec?'

'Mmm?'

'You remember the card I found on Friday?'

Alec sat up at once, taut as a bow-string. 'Sarah, you're surely not going to bring that up again?'

'Please, Alec, don't be angry. We must talk about it.'

'Why must we? There is nothing whatsoever to be gained by discussing it.'

'I had another one today.'

He stared at her grimly, incredulously. 'Tell me.'

She quickly related to him the day's events and as she talked she could sense his resistance weakening, his attitude changing. I'm convincing him, she thought, he believes me now. '. . . and when I got back to the kitchen, the card was gone,' she finished.

Immediately the reservations were back. 'Gone? Again?'

The implications of 'again?' were unbearable. 'But don't you see, Alec? It was only to be expected, predictable. In fact, I was not at all surprised to find it gone. I expect that that was why I was shut into the workshed, so that he could find the card and remove it again.'

'But why should he want to remove it?'

'To frighten and confuse me even further of course, to make it worse for me by ensuring in this way that I would have no proof to give you, nothing to convince you. Please, Alec, don't you see? You are playing his game.' She clutched at his hands as if the force of her grip would convince him.

'But, Sarah, none of it makes sense. Why should this person, if he exists, want to frighten you?' His tone was soothing, reasonable, implacable.

'What do you mean, if he exists?' She stood up abruptly. 'You don't believe me, do you? You don't believe any of it. Why? I don't usually tell lies, do I?' Alec's shake of the head exasperated her beyond the point of self-control, and she screamed at him, 'Then why should I be telling them now? I don't know why it is happening – it just is, I tell you. And you won't believe a word I say.'

Alec stood up too. 'Calm down, Sarah. Calm down, and we'll talk about it.' And he tried to put his arms around her.

She shook him off. 'What's the point? You'll never believe me. But it happened, really happened, just as I told you.'

Alec's arms fell to his sides and stayed there, curiously rigid. 'Then where is the proof?' he said, coldly.

Sarah stared at him, aghast. Their eyes met and locked, but they were the eyes of strangers, devoid of warmth and understanding. She could bear it no longer and, turning, she ran blindly out of the room. She laboured up the stairs, clinging on to the banisters, tears of anger, disappointment and despair dimming her vision. She had expected an argument, but nothing like this. How could he disbelieve her? Why should he think that she was making it all up?

She paused at the nursery door for comfort, but found none. Was the baby, so much desired, to come to a divided home? The memory of herself screaming at Alec, of his cold, implacable stare, drove her across the landing to their own room and flung her, sobbing still, on to the bed.

Suddenly, Alec was beside her, soothing, calming. 'Hush, Sarah, hush. You'll harm yourself, and the baby, if you go on like this. Darling, I can't bear to see you like this. I do love you. Please stop . . .'

Reconciliation was sweet. It was the worst quarrel they had ever had and afterwards neither of them dared to bring up the subject which had caused it. They had had arguments before, of course, but nothing like this, and they had both been too alarmed by the rift which had opened between them at that moment in the sitting-room to have sufficient courage to mention the things which were uppermost in their minds, but which had brought it about. In bed that night they went to sleep with their arms around each other, physically close, but mentally as far apart as it was possible for them to be.

Next morning they were careful, polite, conciliatory. Sarah fetched Alec's coat and briefcase for him, Alec got Sarah's car out for her, in readiness for her visit to Mary that morning. It seemed as though they were both saying that they cared about each other, were willing to put themselves out and give in terms of both time and trouble, but that neither was willing to concede on the matter of the strange occurrences. Sarah knew they had taken place, Alec didn't believe that they had, and that was that.

But what, Sarah asked herself after Alec had gone, can he think I am doing? Does he think that I have deliberately made all this up, or does he think I am imagining it all? Each alternative was equally unpleasant, and it was with relief that she set out for Mary's house. Mary would believe her, she was sure. As she drove along her spirits lifted a little and it was with eagerness that she swung the car into the road where her friend lived.

It was a pleasant cul-de-sac of some twenty houses, built six years previously on the site of a Victorian house which had been pulled down to make way for them. David, who taught history, had at that time just secured the post of Head of Department at a nearby comprehensive school, and the promotion had, after much heart-searching, encouraged him to buy one of these houses. Detached, and with a pleasantly large garden, it was a much nicer house than their previous semi-detached, and they had since been relieved that they had taken the plunge when they had; the prices of such houses had risen so steeply since then that they would never have been able to afford one had they waited.

Mary was obviously looking out for her, and as Sarah's car pulled up in front of the house she waved from the window and disappeared. Sarah picked up her coat and bag from the seat beside her, and by the time she had opened the door, Mary was coming down the path to greet her. Sarah felt a rush of relief and gratitude at the sight of Mary's solid, comforting figure, her placid, smiling face, the heavy, fair hair drawn back and knotted at the back of her neck.

Sarah flung her coat over her arm and Mary at once stooped to pick something up. 'You've dropped something, Sarah.' And straightening up: 'How are you?' Then: 'What's the matter?'

Sarah was staring at the small square of pasteboard in Mary's hand.

'Sarah, what is it? You look as though you've seen a ghost.'

Taking the card from Mary's outstretched hand, Sarah forced a smile. 'Perhaps I have. Let's go in.'

They walked up the path to the house, Mary shooting concerned glances at Sarah's tight, unsmiling face, Sarah not daring to look at the card until they were inside the house. Although she kept her eyes averted from it, she was acutely conscious of the feel of it between her fingers, the smooth, slightly slippery surface, the lethal smallness of it. She felt shaken. She had thought that she would be prepared the next time she received one, that she had in some measure come to terms with the fact that someone was deliberately setting out to frighten her. She must still be even more shaken than she had realized by the disagreement with Alec, and this had caused the card to upset her more than she had thought it would.

She became aware that Mary was fussing around

54

her, settling her on the settee. She smiled gratefully up at her. 'I'm all right, really I am.'

'Well, you don't look it. Whatever is the matter?'

Sarah held out the card. She still hadn't looked at it. 'This.'

Mary looked mystified, but took the card and read aloud what was written on it. ' "Life for life, eye for eye, tooth for tooth, hand for hand, foot for foot, burning for burning, wound for wound, stripe for stripe. Exodus twenty-one, twenty-three".' She looked up. 'What on earth does it mean?'

Sarah shook her head. 'I wish I knew. It's the third one I've had.'

'All the same?'

'No, a different message on each.' Suddenly she started to cry, burying her face in her hands. Mary's arm around her shoulders, her voice soothing her, recalled all the times when she had been desperately unhappy at school, when Mary's reassuring presence had enabled her to pull herself together and put a brave face on it. Gradually she calmed down and began to tell her story, disjointedly at first, then more coherently as her tears abated and she felt more in command of herself. When she had finished, Mary's first question was: 'What does Alec make of it?'

Sarah looked down at her hands, twisting her handkerchief in her lap. 'He thinks I am making it up, or imagining it.' She heard Mary's swift intake of breath. 'We had a dreadful quarrel about it.'

Mary was clearly nonplussed. She knew them both well enough to realize that real quarrels were rare between them and to know how much this would have affected Sarah. 'No wonder you're so upset. Look, I'll go and make some coffee while you sit there for a few minutes, then we'll really thrash this out. There must be an explanation.' She patted Sarah comfortingly on the arm and went into the kitchen.

Sarah immediately felt better. What a relief it was to be believed! She grew calmer by the minute and by the time Mary came back with the coffee she was feeling relatively cheerful.

Mary gave her a searching glance. 'That's better.' She handed Sarah her cup of coffee and sat down. 'You're quite sure you can't think of anybody who could be doing this – someone you might have hurt, offended, insulted? No? I must say I can't see you doing any of those things, not intentionally at any rate.' She sat up. 'That's a thought. Perhaps you've hurt someone unintentionally?'

Sarah shook her head again, more emphatically. 'It's no good, Mary. I've thought and thought about it. I've done little else but think about it, but I just can't come up with an answer. I know one can hurt people without realizing it, but surely not to this extent. This person must really hate me.'

There was a long pause while they both struggled to make sense of it all, then Sarah shrugged. 'I did wonder, for a while yesterday, if it could have been Mr Turner, but I simply can't see that he has any possible motive.'

'He might want his house back?'

'He'd never be willing to pay the market price. Anyway, I think he's quite happy in his caravan.'

'I agree, it does seem rather far-fetched. In any case, I feel there's something much more personal in all this.'

Sarah shivered. 'I know. That's what terrifies me.'

'Have you discussed going to the police?'

'No. I couldn't say that we've ever discussed the subject at all. The very mention of it sends Alec up in the air. And I couldn't go to the police unless he agreed to it, however hard-pressed I was, especially without a shred of evidence.'

'You have this card now,' and Mary nodded towards where it still lay on the low table in front of the settee.

56

'So I have.' Sarah picked it up and put it carefully into the pocket of her maternity dress. 'I won't let it out of my sight.'

'Perhaps when Alec sees it he'll change his mind.'

'I hope so.' But Sarah's tone was sceptical, and the thought of yet another argument shrivelled her soul. She rose to go. 'Anyway, I can't begin to tell you what a relief it's been to talk about it.'

Mary sighed and shook her head. 'I only wish I could have come up with a possible explanation.' She paused with her hand on the front door knob. 'Don't let it go on indefinitely without doing anything about it, will you? And give me a ring any time you like.'

Sarah stepped out on to the porch ahead of her. 'Thanks, I will. Which mornings are you teaching?'

'Monday, Wednesday and Thursday.'

'Fine.' Sarah was very conscious of the fact that across the road someone was watching them from the shadowy depths of her sitting-room. 'Mrs Arthur is at it again.' She waved, and the figure disappeared.

'I know. It's infuriating, isn't it? She's bored and lonely, I suppose.'

'That doesn't make it any more pleasant for you.' Sarah thought, as she had so often thought before, that she would hate to live here, to have no real privacy. Admittedly it was curiosity not malice which drove most of the people in a street like this to take an interest in the comings and goings of their neighbours, but she felt, still raw from her experiences of the last few days, that it would nevertheless be unbearable to have every action scrutinized and interpreted by someone else. 'I'll see you tomorrow evening, then.'

'Tomorrow evening? Oh yes, Angela's. I didn't know that you and Alec were coming. Did you run out of excuses?'

'Don't be horrid.' Sarah smiled shamefacedly. 'Alec

has made me change my mind about Angela. At least, I think he has.'

'Oh, in what way?'

'Well, you know how I've always felt about Angela?' Sarah plucked a leaf from the dome of golden privet beside the front gate and began to shred it. 'How she makes me feel so small because she seems so marvellous in every possible way?'

Mary laughed. 'I think she makes us all feel a bit like that.'

'Alec thinks that she always has to make herself better than other women because she's terrified that, if she doesn't, she'd lose Frank.'

'He may well be right. Poor girl. It must be hell to have a philanderer for a husband. It might do him a lot of good if she retaliated in some way – walked out on him, or threw dishes at him or something. I suppose she's afraid that, if she did, he might leave her for good.'

Sarah manoeuvred herself into the car. 'I suppose so. Anyway, I feel I've been unfair to her. We'll see how things go tomorrow.' She started the engine and put the car into gear. 'And thanks again.'

As she drove off she felt full of gratitude for Mary's unquestioning acceptance of her strange story. At the same time she felt a mixture of guilt and resentment towards Alec, guilt because she felt disloyal at having revealed his attitude to Mary, and resentment that he had not immediately accepted the truth of what she had told him, as Mary had. He should, she felt, be the one person above all others on whom she should be able to rely when she needed help, and he had let her down.

The appearance of the third card this morning had seemed so inevitable that it was only now that it occurred to her to wonder how it had found its way into her coat. The car had been standing outside, unlocked, since early morning, but her coat had not been inside it. She had carried it out with her when she was ready to leave. Then she remembered that, just before she drove off, she had realized that she had not taken out of the deep-freeze the chicken which she intended cooking for supper. It would have been too late to defrost it by the time she got back at lunch-time, so she had got out of the car and gone back into the house to take it out of the freezer before leaving. She hadn't been inside the house more than a few minutes, and she shivered as she realized once again what a close surveillance this implied.

Suddenly she became aware that the rattle was back in the engine. It was not a loud noise and not really a matter for concern, as it had been making itself heard intermittently for months now. It seemed more persist-ent this time, though, and she decided to call in at the garage on the way home so that Bill could hear it before it disappeared again.

When she arrived in the village, it was irritating to find the garage closed. She had forgotten that it was past twelve o'clock, when Bill always closed for lunch. She would ring him this afternoon.

But after lunch she felt deathly tired, as though the mere prospect of doing anything at all were too much for her, and she decided to have a long rest. She had had so many disturbed nights lately, and so many distressing experiences, that she felt she needed a period of unbroken sleep to refresh herself.

She checked that all the doors were securely locked, then mounted the stairs wearily to her bedroom, taking the card with her. She put it under her pillow, reflecting that nothing, absolutely nothing, was going to prevent her from showing Alec this one. She rarely took a rest in the afternoon, but when she did she never found any difficulty in going to sleep. It was as if the fact that there was no real urgency about whether she slept or not, that there were no long hours of darkness in which to lie awake listening despairingly to the ticking of the clock, made it possible for her to relax. This afternoon, however, she was very conscious of the card beneath her pillow. Its presence in her bed was somehow obscene, a jarring, discordant note which kept her awake. It seemed a long time before she drifted away into the oblivion she so sorely needed.

The oblivion, however, was not as comforting as it should have been. She dreamed that she was running after Alec down an endless corridor. Her feet, as so often in dreams, seemed heavy, weighted, to be moving in slow motion. She knew that she would never catch up with him. She was crying, calling out to him, and she awoke with the tears wet upon her cheeks and the sound of his receding footsteps in her ears. In the distance she heard a faint click. She knew it well. It was the sound of the front door shutting.

She sat up, her heart pounding. Could she have imagined it? She was sure that she hadn't. In that case . . . She got heavily out of bed and hurried across to the window. There was nobody to be seen on the drive below, in the garden or out on the road. Defeatedly she got back into bed, still somewhat disorientated from sleep. Already the nightmare had faded and she was left with only the memory of distress. She could, however, clearly recall the distinctive sound made by the front door as it closed.

She leaned back against the pillows and stared bleakly at the opposite wall. The knowledge that the intruder had been able to get into the house when it had been securely locked up added a new dimension to her fears. There was little comfort in trying to reassure herself that he meant her no physical harm, that if he intended to attack her he could never hope to have a better opportunity than the one he had just passed by. The thought that a malignant presence was able to come and go in the house at will made her shrink inwardly. Impelled by the need for some kind of protest against such an intolerable situation she got out of bed again and began to dress. She would get the locks changed at once. Slipping the card into her pocket, she hurried downstairs to the telephone.

It took her twenty minutes of pleas and blandishments to get a locksmith to agree that yes, he would come at once, this afternoon, and change them. She didn't know what Alec would say, she only knew that she felt quite unable to stay in the house now without the added security of different locks. She would just have to brave his displeasure as best she could. She went into the kitchen and stood leaning against the table, mentally exhausted by the effort of persuading the locksmith to immediate action, and closed her eyes in despair at the thought of the scene there would be when Alec arrived home.

After a few minutes, restlessness drove her back into the sitting-room. She rang the garage and arranged to drop her car in on the way home from her relaxation class next morning, then stood drumming her fingers on the telephone table and wondering what she could do to fill in the time until the locksmith arrived. Now that she knew the watcher could get into the house whenever he wished she felt trapped, like a fly in a web awaiting the approach of the spider. She decided to go out into the garden where at least she would have space about her.

Outside, the fresh air and warmth of the sun met her like a benediction. She breathed in deeply, turning up her face to the sunshine, then set off on a leisurely tour of the garden. She inspected the roses at the front of the house, wandered across the terrace which ran along the west side of the house, and continued across the lawn and through the pergola which surrounded it into the wild part of the garden.

Here the grass was left rough, cut only occasionally with a rotary mower. This area had originally been part of the orchards which still surrounded the house on two sides, and here stood the apple trees which Mr Turner had stripped that first autumn. At some time in the past a previous owner had obviously decided to incorporate part of the orchard into the garden and had marked the dividing line with a hawthorn hedge. This had been neglected in the early stages of its growth and had grown tall and leggy, with large gaps between the base of the plants. Sarah and Alec had cut it back hard in the hope that it would thicken up, but the damage had been done and the gaps at the base had remained.

Eventually, the previous autumn, they had bought a quantity of young hawthorn bushes and planted them in the gaps. Sarah decided that she would make a tour of the perimeter of the garden and inspect the progress of the young plants. She would have plenty of time. It should be at least another twenty minutes before the locksmith arrived.

She started at the point where the hedge began, half-way up the west side of the garden, and worked steadily along to the point where this hedge met the one along the north side. Continuing eastwards she had moved along perhaps two-thirds of its length when she came to an abrupt halt. Here, at last, was evidence, real and irrefutable. At this point a number of the new bushes had been broken, trampled down. A gap in the hedge had been enlarged, and there was a clearly defined path leading into the orchard on the other side.

Chapter Seven

As she stood staring at the tell-tale track, Sarah's suspicions of Mr Turner whirled around in her head, then fused into certainty. Here before her, surely, was the proof of his guilt. No one could have used a path into his orchard as often as this one had been used without being seen by the fruit farmer, especially at this time of year when there was so much work being done in the orchards.

She bent to examine the opening more closely. It was about eighteen inches wide and four feet high, and the grass was flattened to a distance of about two feet on either side of the hedge. Sarah frowned. It looked as if something heavy had repeatedly been dragged through the opening. What could it have been? She fingered one of the small, broken hawthorn bushes at the side of the gap. From the point where the main stem had snapped the uppermost twigs still dangled, and the wood at the breaking-point was still green, the leaves only just beginning to shrivel where they hung. The damage, then, was comparatively recent. Probably in the last week or two.

Sarah's forehead creased in concentration as she tried to remember when Alec had last cut this area of rough grass. If there had been anything amiss at that time he would surely have noticed it. It must have been on the Saturday of the weekend before last. At this time of year the grass was not growing very vigorously, and she remembered his remarking that he hoped it might be the last cut of the season.

As she crouched awkwardly, fingers still absent-mindedly smoothing the broken stem of the little shrub, bent head almost touching the main hedge which rose up above her, her eyes, glazed in thought, suddenly focused on something hidden in the foliage, only a few inches in front of them. Putting out her hand, she held back the leaves which obscured her view. It was a piece of green string which had been carefully tied round one of the branches of the main hedge to hold it out of the way and enlarge the opening.

Rising clumsily to her feet, Sarah bent to examine the other side of the opening. Yes, there was a further branch tied back on that side. Clearly Mr Turner's intention was that, when he had no further use for the opening, he would untie the branches and restore the hedge as closely as possible to its original condition.

At this moment she became aware of an impatient hooting from the drive. The locksmith must have arrived and obviously was not too pleased at being kept waiting. She hurried towards the front garden, preoccupied with what she had just seen. She still could not think of any possible reason why Mr Turner should have embarked on this sinister campaign, but there was a tremendous sense of thankfulness in her that now Alec would have to believe her. There was no way of explaining away that deliberately contrived path through the hedge.

As it happened, however, when he arrived home explanations were not necessary. Sarah was hovering in the sitting-room, keeping a look out for him. She wanted to open the front door for him so that she would be able to distract his attention from the new lock until she had had an opportunity to make her explanations. She felt keyed up, prepared for the worst, but determined that this time she would not be prevented from saying all that she had to say by her usual fear of Alec's displeasure. It was, by now, too serious for that. She felt that if she did not from now on have his support in this affair, she would not be able to cope any longer. Her mind refused to consider what would happen to her if he still did not believe her. She only knew that the possibility was something she dared not contemplate.

As the time of his arrival drew closer she felt a hollowness at the pit of her stomach, a churning apprehension, and when the familiar blue Cortina swung into the drive she closed her eyes momentarily and took a deep breath to steady herself before going to open the door.

Alec's movements were slow, as if he, too, were preoccupied. With a stab of guilt she realized that she had been so engrossed with her own predicament that, since that first evening, she had not even bothered to mention the collection which meant so much to him, and which would in normal circumstances have figured so largely in their life at the moment. He had not realized that she was waiting for him at the door and slowly, automatically, he locked the car, shut the garage doors and picked up his briefcase.

He hesitated still, looking at the ground, and for one disconcerting moment it was as if Sarah saw him through the eyes of a stranger, a tall, drooping, middle-aged man with thinning hair. Then, as quickly as this alien vision had come, it vanished, and she was looking at Alec again, the tall, strong, familiar Alec she loved so much. He's afraid to come in, she thought. He doesn't know what he'll find. Another hysterical scene, perhaps. Her heart contracted with pity, fear, love, compunction, and she stepped out of the doorway and called his name in a low voice.

He looked up and saw her standing there, his face clearing as he saw her smile. In a few strides he was before her, his arms were around her. 'Sarah, love, can you forgive me?'

Sarah leant against him, dizzy with relief. It was going to be all right.

'Sarah?' He held her away from him, looking searchingly into her face. 'Come on, let's go in.'

In the kitchen he took her hands. 'Mary rang me this morning.'

So Alec's change of heart had been brought about by somebody else. Resentment rose in her and she shook her head in an involuntary gesture of protest. 'She shouldn't have done that.'

'She was worried about you.'

'She had no right to interfere. It's most unlike her.'

'I'm glad she did. Sarah, forgive me?'

She averted her eyes. She felt acutely uncomfortable. Alec, pleading, was unfamiliar.

'I don't blame you for turning away.'

'But I wasn't. I just didn't know what to say.'

'Sarah, please. I know I've been blind and selfish. You've been worried to death and I've been so wrapped up in my own affairs that I couldn't see it.'

'I've been selfish, too. I know how much the collection means to you.'

'Damn the collection. Do you think that you are not as important to me as a bundle of papers?'

But I'm not, cried Sarah inwardly. I'm not. If I had been, we wouldn't be having this conversation now. 'Of course I am, I know that,' she lied.

Although she had longed to hear Alec say something of the kind over the past few days, Sarah found that she couldn't make herself sound very convincing. He had been selfish; she had needed him. Did he really feel that he had let her down, or was it simply that his ego had been damaged, that he had let himself down in his own eyes as the ever efficient, capable man in control of every situation? She became aware that the silence had become unpleasantly protracted, that Alec was still awaiting some further reassurance from her. As she opened her mouth to give it he turned abruptly away from her.

'For heaven's sake, what do you want me to do – crawl?' He turned to face her again. 'I've said I'm sorry, haven't I?'

'Alec, don't be angry.' Again she felt a spurt of resentment. How had their positions become reversed? Why was she now the one pleading for forgiveness? She reflected bitterly that Alec never remained in an inferior position for long. She should have foreseen this. His face was closed, stony.

'Alec, please. I have been so very unhappy.' The appeal to his protective instincts softened him, as she knew it would. He drew her to him and stroked her hair.

'Poor Sarah. You have had a bad time of it.'

Almost against her will she found herself relaxing against him. It was good not to feel so alone, to feel safe, protected.

'Now, I think we'd better start again. Right from the beginning. I gather there's a lot more than you've told me so far.'

With a complicated pang of feeling compounded of anger at Mary's interference, gratitude for the result of her intervention, scorn at her own capitulation and relief that the disagreement between herself and Alec had been resolved, Sarah pulled away from him and took him by the hand.

'Alec, first there's something I want you to see.'

He followed her wordlessly out into the garden, across the lawn and through the apple trees to the gap in the hedge. She told him how she had come to notice it, pointing out in the fading light the broken plants, the tied-back branches, and they puzzled together over the marks of dragging on the grass in the opening. As they walked back she explained how she had begun to suspect Mr Turner the day before, telling him about the face she had seen peering through the hedge, the subsequent encounter with Mr Turner, the mysteriously open workshed door, the shock she had had on being shut in when she went to investigate. He confirmed that he had not left the door open himself and reacted violently to Sarah's statement of her conviction that the intruder had been inside the house that afternoon while it had been securely locked up.

'We must get the locks changed first thing in the morning.'

'I got it done this afternoon.' For the first time since it all began Sarah felt almost happy. The relief, the sheer relief that Alec believed her, was taking it all seriously, had not been angry about the locks, was sufficient to send her spirits soaring. To have his unqualified support, not to have to face it alone was, at the moment, enough.

During supper, by mutual agreement, they talked of other things, but when they eventually carried their coffee cups into the sitting-room and settled down on the settee, Alec fell into a thoughtful silence.

'What really baffles me is what possible motive Turner, or anybody else for that matter, could have in trying to frighten you. Whichever way I look at it, there seems to be no answer. I wonder . . . can you remember the exact wording of the cards?'

Sarah put her hand into her pocket and took out the one she had had that morning. She gave a small smile of contentment at the thought that she had not needed after all to show it to Alec to convince him, as she had expected. She had shown it to him briefly before supper, while telling her story. 'This is the one that came this morning. As I said, it was in the folds of my coat, on the seat of the car.'

'How could it have got there?'

'I think it must have been put there when I came back into the house for a few minutes. I'd forgotten to take the chicken out of the freezer.'

Alec frowned. Obviously he, too, realized the close degree of observation this implied. 'Have they all been printed, like this?'

'Yes, all in block capitals, on the same sort of card.'

Alec fingered the card. 'That doesn't tell us anything either. It's been cut off a postcard, I would say.' He looked at her. 'Can you remember the wording of the other two?'

'I think so. The first one I remember very clearly. It was: "Boast not thyself of tomorrow: for thou knowest not what a day may bring forth." That's it. I can't remember the verse number, though. I think it was Proverbs, but I'm not sure.'

'What about the other one?'

'Now, let me see.' She paused, sending herself back in time to that moment at the washing-line, the towel in her hand, the sun shining on her back, the card in her hand. Square black letters on a white background. She said it over to herself first, then repeated it aloud to Alec. ' "To everything there is a season, and a time to every purpose under heaven. A time to be born, and a time to die." '

Alec wrote down the words as she said them. He frowned heavily as he came to the last word. 'And then there's this one.' He read it aloud, consideringly. ' "Life for life, tooth for tooth, hand for hand, foot for foot, burning for burning, wound for wound, stripe for stripe." Nasty, very nasty.' He continued to look at the three messages. 'How would you describe their tone?'

Sarah leaned over and read them again in silence. 'I don't know. The only thing *I'm* sure about is that they are warnings of some kind. The implication is that something nasty is going to happen to me. And,' she continued more hesitantly, 'whatever it is, it's connected with the baby.' She felt again the cold clutch of fear and shivered. 'That's what terrifies me.'

Alec looked sharply at her. 'You're not still worried, are you? As you were on Friday?'

For a moment Sarah was tempted to describe to Alec the true extent of her fears. He was in a particularly sympathetic mood and it would ease her of a further burden she had been carrying alone. On the other hand, it might mean that he would be sidetracked and the more pressing matter of the cards might be pushed aside. Swiftly she decided that this was not the moment to complicate the issue. 'I haven't thought about it much, Alec. Not for the last couple of days, anyway.' As she spoke she realized that, astonishingly, this was true. 'I suppose it's still there, underneath. I think most women probably worry at this stage of a pregnancy. But it's not getting on top of me, as it was on Friday.' She recalled her terror of Friday evening, her inability to think of anything but her fear that something would go wrong, that the baby would be still-born or deformed. 'I suppose that in some topsy-turvy fashion I ought to be grateful to whoever it is. He has certainly succeeded in distracting me from that worry.'

'Sarah.' Alec took both her hands. He was, clearly, overcome by remorse again. Sarah could never remember him being so . . . she groped for the word . . . humble, that was it, humble, before. Fleetingly she wondered if Mary had been as tactful and diffident as Alec had seemed to indicate. She was capable of being very forthright when she thought it necessary. She had a sudden vision of Mary admonishing Alec. She had never imagined Alec in a position of weakness before, and did not like it now.

'Sarah!' A much more characteristic hint of impatience in his tone recalled her. 'You're not listening!' There was even a familiar breath of exasperation.

Sarah sat up. 'Sorry, Alec.'

'I was just saying that I think you ought to go and have a word with Doctor Blunsdon.'

'Whatever for?'

'Just to check up that you are all right.'

'Darling, I'm perfectly all right.'

'Well, all this business is very upsetting for you. I think you ought to see him, get him to check your blood pressure and so on.'

'Alec, I'm having a check-up once a week now as a matter of routine. Honestly, I'm fine.' Especially now that you are taking this business seriously, she added to herself.

Alec was clearly reluctant to let the matter go. Obviously he felt so strongly that he had let her down, that he was rather overdoing things in trying to make up for it. It was, thought Sarah with a sudden quirk of amusement, his conscience he needed to take to the doctor, not his wife. She drew his attention back to the verses on the paper in his lap, the card in his hand. 'This one – ' and she touched the latest message – 'is different from the first two in some way.' She considered it, head on one side. 'I know . . . it's more of a threat, somehow.'

'Eye for eye. The classic revenge motif. Of course. How stupid of me not to have seen it before. This one – ' and he flourished the card in his hand – 'this one gives us the motive, the reason for the whole business.'

'Revenge? But Alec, what for? I don't see why you are so excited. I've assumed all along that it must be someone who has a grudge against me for some reason. Otherwise it's all so senseless, so insane.' And again she felt that lurch of fear.

'Yes, but assuming is different from knowing.'

'I still don't see how it helps. What could I possibly have done to Mr Turner, or to anyone else for that

71

matter, that could make them wish to launch a campaign of this extent against me?'

'It does seem far-fetched, I know, but then the whole business is so improbable that any explanation of it is almost bound to be equally so. Come on, darling, think. Have you ever done or said anything which could have upset him, offended him, anything like that?'

Sarah sat and thought. 'No, Alec. Really, I don't think I've ever done more than pass the time of day with him.' She smiled. 'Perhaps it's just the opposite. Perhaps he feels so guilty about pocketing the proceeds from our apples that first year that he can't bear to have me always about as a reminder of his misdeed.'

They both started to laugh. The thought of Mr Turner overcome by pangs of conscience, particularly in relation to a deal by which he had profited financially, was richly amusing.

'Of course,' said Alec, still laughing, 'if it had been the other way around, if we had cheated him, one could just imagine . . .' He stopped laughing abruptly. His expression became thoughtful, speculative. 'I wonder . . .'

'Alec, don't keep me in suspense. What is it?'

'Well, it has just occurred to me. Suppose, just suppose, that he thinks we have cheated him over this house?'

'How could he? He wouldn't budge an inch over the price, you know that. He was paid what he asked for.'

'I know, but look at it from his point of view. Would you say that it was worth more or less than it was when we bought it?'

'More, of course. We've spent over five thousand on it since then. We've put in central heating, had it re-wired, replaced all the bathroom fittings and plumbing, modernized the kitchen . . .'

'Yes, I know all that. We both do, but does he?'

'Well, he must know that we've had a lot done to it.'

'But he, my love, is the sort of man who would never pay out good money to replace something until it disintegrated. He wouldn't think in terms of how much we've spent, only in terms of how much we'd get. And it must be obvious that we would get a great deal more for it now than he did four years ago.'

'I still can't see it, Alec. It doesn't make sense to me.'

'It should, if you think that he is known to be obsessed with making money. Mostly in small ways. A man like that is too small-minded to think on a large scale. That is why it would be all the more galling to him to feel cheated on his one big deal. Here we are, right under his nose all the time, a constant reminder, in his mind, of how much more he would have made if he had waited a few years before selling.'

'You could be right, I suppose,' said Sarah doubtfully.

'I know it's scarcely credible, but then, as I said just now, the whole business is so unbelievable that any explanation is bound to be equally so. And it is the nearest we have come to any explanation at all. You are absolutely certain that you can't think of anyone else who could possibly wish you harm?'

Sarah thought again. The conversation had exhausted her and her head was beginning to ache. She shook her head and, as if he had been waiting for a signal, Alec jumped up.

'That settles it, then.'

Sarah sat up in alarm. 'What do you mean?' What are you doing?'

'Calling the police.'

'No, please, Alec, don't.'

But he already had the telephone in his hand and was dialling. Sarah got up as quickly as she could.

'Alec, no!' The urgency in her voice must have communicated itself to him for he looked up, saw her face and replaced the receiver in its rest. He came slowly towards her. 'What is it? We must call them, you do see that?'

'I know. But not tonight, please, Alec. I feel so tired. I couldn't face going through it all over again tonight. Let's leave it until morning.'

Alec hesitated. 'The morning would be difficult. I have an appointment with Doctor Fellows first thing. I have to give him a preliminary report on the collection. Then there's a meeting with some of the others to map out how the work is to be tackled, who is to be responsible for which aspects of it and so on.'

Sarah felt a faint stirring of resentment but stifled it. Alec had been so patient, so understanding this evening, and it was, after all, her fault that immediate action was not being taken. Perhaps she ought to pull herself together and face the police now? At the thought an immense weariness gripped her. 'Well, let's wait until you come home from work tomorrow.' She didn't want to go alone. It was such a wild tale that the police might think she was just another hysterical, attention-seeking woman. Alec's presence would lend her story credibility.

'I don't think we ought to leave it as long as that.'

'But, Alec, as I said earlier, I don't think any physical harm is intended or he would never have passed by the opportunity this afternoon. I honestly don't think another day will make much difference. I feel so much better now we've talked about it that I shan't in the least mind waiting until the afternoon.' She sagged with the effort of trying to convince him, and he put out his hand to steady her.

'You look all in. All right, then. We'll go as soon as I get home from work. I think you ought to go straight up to bed. Go on, up you go, and I'll bring you a hot drink.'

She let herself be coaxed towards the stairs. At the top, tired as she was, she flicked on the nursery light and stood for a moment looking in. Familiar as her own face in the mirror, it gazed serenely back at her. She turned away, smiling. For the moment, all was well. She had been granted a reprieve.

Chapter Eight

'Clench your right fist and contract the muscles in your right arm, please. Now begin your breathing in position one. Breathe in through your nose, slowly, blow out through your mouth. In . . . out, in . . . out, one more before going up into position two. In . . . out. Now up into position two. Mouth slightly open. In . . . out. Make sure you can feel your rib-cage expanding. In . . . out, in . . . out.'

As the voice of the midwife gave her instructions Sarah tried to achieve the necessary state of total concentration, to focus her awareness on nothing but causing the breath to enter and leave her body in the right way, following the correct rhythm. All around her other women, also in the advanced stages of pregnancy, lay in the same position as she, shoulders raised on pillows into a semi-sitting position, knees drawn up and wide apart.

Like the swimming sessions, her attendance at these natural childbirth classes had been inspired by a photograph, this time in one of the reputable Sunday papers. It had shown a woman actually giving birth. She had been half-lying, half-sitting, in the same position as Sarah was now, but it had been the look on her face which had really impressed itself on Sarah's mind. She had been smiling, a wide, delighted, spontaneous smile. All the tales of suffering in childbirth, the centuries-long traditions of pain had melted away before that smile, and Sarah had never forgotten it. She had been in her early teens then, but the image of that astounding photograph had stored itself away in her mind and when she found she was pregnant she had made enquiries and found that relaxation classes were held as an adjunct to the ante-natal clinic she attended.

Later, she realized how lucky she had been. The nurse in charge, Nurse Hills, was an instructor trained by the Natural Childbirth Trust, and had herself borne a child by this method. The memory of that photograph, together with the knowledge that this woman had experienced what she, Sarah, was to experience and had found this method really worked, had given her a tremendous confidence in the training and a determination to fulfil it as well as she possibly could.

'. . . and relax. Thank you, ladies, that will be all for today. Except that this time, before you go, there are one or two things I must say to you.'

There was a general shifting into more comfortable positions amongst the members of the class as they settled down to listen. Nurse Hills hesitated before she began, as if marshalling her thoughts.

'Most of you here will have your babies during the next few weeks, and before you do, there are one or two points that I must mention again, though most of them have come up at one time or another during the last few months. First of all, I know that this method works, because I have experienced it. I had two children by conventional methods and one by this, and I can assure you that the difference cannot be believed unless it is experienced.

'This method really works, I repeat, and it does so because it frees the womb to get on with its work of pushing the baby out into the world without anything hindering it or making its work difficult.

'During labour, the disengaging exercises you have practised with different groups of muscles in the body

77

are transferred to the womb, and during the contractions you experience your breathing enables you to remain completely relaxed and let the womb get on with its job.'

She smiled at the attentive faces upturned towards her. 'The nearest parallel I can draw is with surfing. Your breathing carries you up on the crest of the wave of the contraction, then down the other side. But the important thing is that you are on top of the wave, not drowning in it. You, not the contraction, are in control. Discomfort there will be, but not pain. You will find that women who have had babies in the ordinary way will scoff at this idea, but I can assure you that it is true. I repeat, I know because I have experienced it myself.

'But I must end with two notes of caution. The first is this. There are circumstances in which, through no fault of your own, you will have to have help. You might even have to be unconscious at the time of the birth. Now, I know how much you are all hoping this will not happen, and I must emphasize that such circumstances are rare. But, if they do occur, don't blame yourself, or feel that you have failed. It won't be your fault.

'The final piece of advice I have to offer is this, and it applies particularly to those of you who are having first babies. Those who use this method and who have had babies before rarely fail because they know what to expect. They don't use up their reserves too quickly. Those who have first babies and find that this method is not adequate, fail because, medical circumstances such as I have just mentioned apart, they go up into each level of breathing too soon, and find they have nothing to fall back on. So, above all, remember this. Don't go up into any level of breathing until you absolutely must, in order to stay in control.

'That's all. And good luck.'

The rapt attention accorded her dissolved into chatter as the dozen or so women prepared to leave. Sarah wondered which of them she might meet in hospital, how many of them would experience that singular happiness of the woman she had seen in the photograph, when it actually came to the birth of their babies. Would she? She ardently hoped that she would, and she left, trying to fix in her mind all that Nurse Hills had just said.

At the bottom of the steps outside the hospital she stopped and looked at her watch. Ten thirty. She suddenly realized that, for the last hour, she had not once thought about the unpleasant situation which awaited her at home. She felt that she couldn't face going back to it, not yet. She would have to be back before twelve, to see Bill and leave her car with him before he stopped work for lunch, but there was no need to go home yet. She would have some coffee in town first.

In the restaurant she felt as though she had awoken to normality from a nightmare. At most tables two or more chattering women, bulging carrier bags on the floor beside them, enjoyed a brief gossip before returning to their shopping. There were one or two tables where women sat alone, but Sarah did not have enough courage to ask permission to share a table with one of them. Her fear of a rebuff was too strong. She had often felt how much she missed in life, by being unable to be at her ease in casual contacts of this kind, and as she sat alone, sipping her coffee, she reflected sadly that it was no use, nothing could change her nature, she might as well resign herself to comparative solitude.

Apart from Alec, Mary was the only close friend she had. She had never found it easy to make friends. She had never really been able to feel that she had anything of value to offer in a friendship, and even with Mary she had always felt that it was Mary's generosity of heart, not any satisfaction she could offer, which had caused Mary to take an interest in her in the first place. Never, in all her life, she thought, had she been in a position of strength in any relationship. She always seemed to be the weak one, the dependent one, the suppliant; the asker, not the giver. Perhaps this was one of the reasons why the baby meant so much to her. For once she would be the strong one, the protector. She would be able to give, as she had never been able to give before.

'Now look what you've done!' The voice, harsh and strident, cut across her thoughts. At the next table sat a young woman and her small daughter, a toddler exquisitely dressed in a scarlet pinafore dress and a deliciously feminine frilly white broderie anglaise blouse. Down the front of the blouse was a spreading orange stain. The mother scrubbed at it with a handkerchief. Her vicious anger, barely contained, showed in the violence of the movement. Sarah shrank inwardly on behalf of the child, as she imagined what the mother's reaction would have been in private. On the child's diminutive features was an expression of indifference. She doesn't care, thought Sarah in horror. She is so used to her mother's anger that she has cut herself off from it. If she let herself care it would hurt too much, so she has stopped caring.

She forced herself to look away. Never, she vowed, never would she treat her child like that. He would have to be disciplined, of course, but she would always try to remember that he was a person, with feelings of his own. This was something which adults seemed so easily to forget. The damage done to herself by the indifference of her own parents was something she would never outgrow, a crippling legacy of lack of confidence and self-esteem.

'Is there anyone sitting here?'

Sarah started. She had been so engrossed in her thoughts that she had not seen the woman approach.

She recognized her at once. It was one of the other women from the relaxation class. Hardly a woman, a girl really, she amended, as she smilingly shook her head and invited her to sit down. 'I've seen you at relaxation class, haven't I?'

'Yes.' The girl drooped, then looked up with a curiously hopeful expression. 'When's your baby due?' The voice was nasal, with an underlying whine to it.

'November the twentieth. And yours?'

'November the fifth. Won't be able to forget his birthday, if he arrives on time, will I? I mean, giving birth amongst the fireworks, bangs, fizzes, explosions, I mean, will I?'

Sarah smiled. 'I suppose not.'

The girl was very young. Perhaps not more than seventeen. Just a child really. She was very thin, too. Her small pinched face had an unhealthy pallor to it, her long dark hair, though clean, hung limply on her shoulders, her gaudy maternity dress was skimpy and badly made. Poor child. She looked singularly ill-equipped for motherhood. Her swollen belly was incongruous, almost obscene beneath that childish, immature face. Something of the sympathy Sarah felt must have shown in her face, for the girl edged her chair closer and glanced around as if to check that they were not being overheard before lowering her voice confidentially.

'Here, d'you mind if I ask you something?'

'Of course not.'

'Well, I haven't liked to ask anyone before. Well, I mean, it's awkward, like, isn't it?'

Sarah had no idea what the girl meant, but nodded encouragingly. Suddenly, it was important to understand. The girl needed something from her. She remembered what she had been thinking a few minutes earlier. Perhaps, this time, she did have something to give. She focused all her attention on what was being said.

'. . . there's only Mum, see. And she's no good. Well, I mean, she's different, isn't she? Old, and that. And I'm the eldest, see, so there's no one else. I haven't got a sister or nothing. And I seen you over here and I thought, I'll ask her. Well, I mean, you're older, aren't you? Not old, like, but older'n me.'

Sarah could only nod again. What could she say? She supposed the girl's meaning would emerge eventually. She steeled herself. All this beating about the bush could mean only one thing. The girl was embarrassed. What could she be leading up to? Her imagination sped wildly from one bizarre explanation to the next, but the question, when it came, floored her completely, took her breath away. She looked at the girl in something like horror. 'What . . . what did you say?'

Fortunately the girl's diffidence at asking her question had kept her from looking at Sarah's face. She sat now, still looking down at her hands which were tightly clenched in her lap, beneath the protuberance of her stomach. 'I said, are you afraid, like?'

How could she know, how could this child know that, despite her oft-repeated reassurances to herself and to Alec that the watcher meant her no physical harm, Sarah was, underneath, desperately, screamingly afraid?

Unaware of Sarah's inner turmoil, the girl was still speaking. 'I mean, I can't believe her, can I? My mother. I mean, she always blows everything up bigger'n it is. She's the best, the prettiest, the men go mad for her, all the things that happen to her are more exciting than what happens to everyone else. See what I mean?' She shot a brief, unseeing glance at Sarah.

'So, having babies, of course, she had the worst time that anyone ever had. I mean, it was hell on earth, the agony, the screams, the pain. That's why I went to the classes. But I still don't know, do I? I mean, how can I until it's happening? And it's soon. Only a few days now. You see what I mean, don't you? I mean, can we believe what she told us?' She jerked her head in the direction of the hospital and Nurse Hills as her voice trailed away.

As she spoke Sarah felt immense relief. The thought that her inmost feelings had been so obvious that even this child had perceived them had horrified her. How stupid she had been to think that it could have been so! All the same she felt shaken. Her misinterpretation of the girl's question had given her an unpleasant piece of self-knowledge; she was much more frightened than she had previously admitted even to herself.

As all this sped through her mind she made a determined effort to put it aside. She would have plenty of time to think of herself later. The girl had moved, now that the worse part was over, and was leaning anxiously forward on the table, looking sideways up into Sarah's face, awaiting her response. Impulsively Sarah put her hand over that of the girl. The thin, immature feel of it, the bitten nails and torn quicks, aroused her compassion still further. How best to reassure her? 'Look – I'm sorry, I don't even know your name . . .'

'Samantha. Samantha Allen.'

'And I'm Sarah Royd. Look, Samantha – I hope you don't mind if I call you that – perhaps it might help if I tell you why I believe in this way of having babies?'

Samantha's eager nod encouraged her to continue. She told her about the photograph she had seen when she was younger than Samantha now was, how she had been so impressed by the joy on the woman's face that she had remembered it all these years – 'about fifteen years, because I'm twenty-eight now' – how her belief in Natural Childbirth had been verified and strengthened by Nurse Hills' own experience, and how she really believed implicitly that if one did all the things they had been instructed to do they would, except in very unusual circumstances, find the experience of childbirth one of the happiest of their lives.

When she had finished Samantha sat in silence for some moments, mulling over what she had heard. Sarah waited, anxiously. Had she succeeded? What an impossible task it was, to reverse in a few minutes the teachings of a lifetime!

Finally, the girl raised her head. 'It was a real photograph, you say?'

'Yes, in one of the finest newspapers in the world. It couldn't possibly have been a fake. It was real, all right.'

'Well, they say the camera never lies, don't they? And what's good enough for you ought to be good enough for me, didn't it? Thanks, Mrs Royd.'

But behind this convincing display Sarah could sense that the doubts still lurked. Nothing, ultimately, would convince the girl but experiencing a painless labour herself, and unfortunately her doubts would probably prevent her from doing so. It was, Sarah knew, essential to have confidence in it for the method to work. Anyway, she had done her best. There was nothing more she could do. She glanced at her watch. 'Look at the time! I shall have to go, I'm afraid.'

'I wish we was going to be in at the same time.' There was a hint of desperation in Samantha's voice which held Sarah pinned to her chair.

'That's not very likely, I'm afraid,' she said gently. She racked her brains for some further reassurance she could give. 'Look, I'll think about you on the fifth and ring up to enquire about you. And if you like, I could come and see you while you're in,' she promised recklessly. Anything to mitigate the bleakness in the girl's eyes.

'Would you? Would you, really?'

'I will, I promise. Now, I'm afraid I really must go.

84

Don't forget, do everything you've learnt in the classes and you'll be fine.' She wondered despairingly as she rose just how much Samantha would have absorbed of what she had been taught. 'And if I were you, I'd try either not to see too much of your mother in the next week, or tell her you don't want to hear another word about her agonizing experiences in labour.'

Suddenly a smile lit up the pale face and for a moment Sarah saw what a pretty girl was hidden behind the fears, and why Samantha had been snapped up in marriage the minute it was legal for her to be so.

'That's a smashing idea. I just thought of a way I could make her stop. I hope I haven't made you late.'

'No, of course you haven't. Good-bye, then, and try not to worry.'

As Sarah crossed the restaurant towards the cash desk she was conscious of Samantha's eyes on her back. She turned to wave. She was right; the girl was watching her, hungrily. She hesitated. Perhaps she should have arranged to see her again before the fifth. The despondent droop of Samantha's head as she turned again to her coffee almost made Sarah go back and suggest it but she was, despite her denial, already late and would have to hurry to catch Bill before he closed for lunch. Nevertheless, a distinct feeling of guilt accompanied her to the car and she shook it off, angrily. She had tried, hadn't she? Worried as she was, she had tried. She had done her best: no one could do more than that.

In her preoccupation she was half-way home before she realized to her annoyance that the rattle had again disappeared. How infuriating it was! As if it had some perverse will of its own, the car always seemed to sense when it was going to the garage. One of these days it would let her down badly, leave her stranded somewhere inaccessible. She toyed with the idea of cancelling the arrangement, then remembered how

85

much worse than usual the noise had been the day before. There must be something wrong. She would let Bill look at it today and if he couldn't find anything she would give up and ignore it until the car broke down.

She reached the garage just in time. Bill was just closing the heavy sliding doors when she pulled in to the forecourt and he came across, wiping his hands on an oily rag.

'Sorry I'm late, Bill. I was held up in town.'

'That's all right, Mrs Royd. I wasn't going to work on her until this afternoon anyway. Just so long as I've got the keys. Would you like me to run you home?'

'No, thanks, Bill, I'll walk. It's such a lovely day, the exercise will do me good.' She glanced at her few purchases on the front seat. 'Will my shopping be in your way?'

'No, not at all.'

'I'll leave it where it is, then. I hope you find out what is causing that rattle, this time. I'm afraid it's stopped again.'

Bill laughed, showing a row of surprisingly even white teeth. 'What did you expect? We'll see what we can do anyway.'

'What time shall I pick it up?'

'You needn't come for it. Young Mick and I have got to go and pick up a customer's car this afternoon. We'll drop it in on the way.'

'Thank you, Bill. See you later, then.'

She walked away across the forecourt, suddenly conscious of the midday heat reflected up at her from the concrete. A few bedding plants, planted at the beginning of the summer, were still trying to bloom in the little beds which Bill tried to keep looking attractive. The long, hot summer, however, had taken its toll and blown by the hot poisonous gusts from innumerable exhaust pipes, smothered by the dust thrown up by

86

countless cars, it was a miracle that they had survived at all. Sarah stopped for a moment to look at them and marvel at their tenacity.

As she continued on her way the diminishing distance between herself and home forced her once more to open her mind to the thoughts she had been keeping at bay all morning. The effect was as if she had been mentally leaning against a closed door with a tremendous pressure on the other side. The moment she stopped doing so the door burst open and she halted abruptly on the road as the torrent hit her. The cards, the strange and frightening events of the last few days, the fears, the speculations rushed through her mind in a confused and terrifying roar.

She put her hands to her head to shut it out, and gradually normality reasserted itself. The country lane, the brown autumn leaves at her feet, the cloudless sky, the glowing colours of the hedgerows materialized before her as if some divine conjuror had produced them especially for her benefit. She felt curiously empty, drained of thought and feeling. Automatically she started walking again. Suddenly she was filled with nostalgia for all the times she had walked this way before, looking forward with a delicious anticipation to the moment when she would turn the bend and the house would come into view. Sometimes she had been unable to prevent herself from running those last few steps.

One of the reasons why it meant so much to her was because it helped her to remember her father with gratitude rather than with bitterness. With his death had finally come the end to her dreams that one day he would grow to love her. She had pinned her hopes on the belief that, given time to recover from the loss of her mother, he might perhaps turn at last to her. But he never had, and although she continued to hope for a miracle, Sarah's love had eventually withered and soured. Like the woman who finds it harder to bear being rejected for herself than to lose her lover to another woman, she had found it bitter indeed to have to accept that, her mother dead and her chief rival for her father's affections out of the way, her father still had no warmth for her. Although her marriage to Alec had given her a degree of happiness she had never known before, the helpless longing of the child Sarah for her father's affection had dogged Sarah the woman until his death.

But the house, at least, he had given her. He had left surprisingly little money, but it had been enough to buy it and to have the necessary alterations done to it. It had been the only time Sarah had dared do battle with Alec. He had been bitterly opposed to the idea of buying a house with her money, but in the end Sarah, tired of life in a flat and longing for a real home of her own, had won. It had seemed ridiculous to her that she should be expected to stay on in the cramped, poky little rooms when there was money in the bank to buy a house of their own. Once he had capitulated Alec had seemed to forget the arguments they had had about it. Perhaps the unusual and uncharacteristic determination she had shown in this matter had convinced him of its importance to her, or perhaps the fact that it had been he who had, in the end, found the house, had reconciled him to her paying for it. All the same she still wondered sometimes if he held it against her. He was so proud and independent it seemed extraordinary that he should never once have mentioned it again.

She reached the bend in the lane, and there it was, beyond the untidy jumble of Mr Turner's farm buildings. But she could not look at it now with pleasure, with anticipation, only with wariness and apprehension. From which direction would the next blow come?

Her shoulders flinched as she stood looking at it, feeling already its force descending upon them.

There was no one about. Mr Turner's yard was totally deserted. She hurried past it, averting her eyes from the ramshackle caravan in the corner. It was past twelve o'clock and he must already have stopped work for lunch. She imagined him sitting in there in squalor, crouched like a toad over his food, shovelling it into his mouth with one eye slyly peering at her through the gap in the curtains beside him. Without looking, she knew that the curtains would be drawn – they always were. All the better to see you with, my dear. She shuddered and kept her face turned away as she scurried past. She wasn't going to give him the satisfaction of seeing that she was upset, afraid, apprehensive.

At her front gate she paused. Here, well away from the main road, the silence was almost tangible. A week ago Sarah would have revelled in the hush which lay upon the house and garden. She remembered how only last Friday, just before her little world had been shattered by that first, innocuous-seeming piece of white card, she had sat at the wheel of her car, soaking in the peace, thankful to be out of the noise and confusion of the busy streets she had just left. How much more she would have relished that moment of tranquillity if she had known that it was to be the last!

Now the silence had a menacing quality, an air of brooding expectancy, and her eyes raked the garden, seeking the outline of a figure crouched in some dark corner, a shadow where there was nothing to cast one. But of course she was being foolish. The shape of her fears was, at the moment, contained in the squalid vehicle parked in the farmyard next door. She opened the gate, latched it behind her and hurried across the drive to the front door. She was about to unlock it when she paused. Perhaps, while he was safely out of the way, she could look again at that peculiar gap in the hedge. There might be something she had missed yesterday, when the locksmith had interrupted her.

She glanced to her right and listened intently. The caravan was, of course, invisible from here, and there were no sounds at all from the other side of the garage where it stood. Surely if he had come out she would have heard? Yesterday afternoon she had been so excited about her discovery that it had not even occurred to her to wonder if he had been watching her. And last night Alec had been with her and she wouldn't have cared anyway.

But this morning, with the noon-day hush about her and the still, hot air imparting a stage-set unreality to the house, the garden, Sarah felt that she must behave with caution. She felt as if she were being forced into playing a part she had no wish to play. The trouble was, she reflected as she set off silently across the terrace, it wasn't a play. It was, if anything, too real, too charged with fear and uneasiness for comfort. She felt that the fact that she was practically tip-toeing across her own garden ought to be funny, but try as she might, she couldn't conjure up even the glimmer of a smile.

The paving slabs beneath her feet had given way to grass, and as she crossed the lawn she relaxed a little and quickened her pace. Driven by an urgency she did not understand and could not control, she emerged through the arch of the pergola into the orchard area at as fast a pace as her ungainly bulk permitted.

She stopped, as suddenly as if she had walked straight into a brick wall. And indeed she felt, mentally, as though she had. Across some thirty yards of rough grass she and Mr Turner caught in the act of picking something up, faced each other, with the expressionless and implacable stare of enemies.

Chapter Nine

For one frozen moment neither of them moved. So convinced had Sarah been that Mr Turner was in his caravan, so vivid her image of him devouring his food, so strong her feeling that he had been watching her as she hurried by, that she could not at first believe the evidence of her eyes. But the stooping figure, still as a carved figurehead, remained, and incredulity turned to panic. What should she do now? For although she had both longed for, yet dreaded, a confrontation, she felt, now that she was faced with one, at a complete loss. To retreat was, in the light of such blatant trespass, unthinkable, but how to deal with the situation was another matter. As if the realization that she must go forward, not back, had penetrated to her legs before her mind had reached a conscious decision, her feet began to move.

The whole episode took on a nightmare quality, and as she approached the inimical figure now straightening itself into an upright position, she felt that she must at any moment wake up, that, as so often happens in dreams, she would never really come face to face with what she feared. Mr Turner's face with its small, bright, acquisitive eyes, its dirt-embedded wrinkles, its lips puckered and turned in upon themselves as if determined to give nothing away, swelled and shrank before her eyes, as if seen in the distorting mirror at a fairground. His tense, wary stance, slightly hunched forward, arms hanging loosely at his sides, fists clenched, seemed to exude a quality of malice which gave him a threatening, predatory air.

Then, suddenly, just before she reached him, there was a sudden change of focus. Sarah blinked, disconcerted. It was as if she had suddenly and miraculously been given a new pair of eyes. The figure of menace had, inexplicably, become merely pathetic, a little old man caught in a guilty act and apprehensive about facing up to the consequences. With her new eyes, Sarah found self-possession. Indignation filled her, but still she did not speak. Slowly and with deliberation she looked about her.

The reason for the track through the hedge was now plain. At the feet of the old man lay a box full of apples. This was why he had been late for lunch. His greed had betrayed him. He hadn't been able to resist filling the box right up. And here, too, was the reason for the dragging marks which had so puzzled her yesterday. Obviously he had not been able to carry the boxes through the gap, it was too low. So he had had to push or pull them through.

She glanced up at the apple tree. The one above her was still laden. Puzzled, her gaze moved on to the next one, then the next. All seemed untouched. Alec intended picking them at the week-end and the heavy boughs drooped over her, their harvest releasing the faint but unmistakable perfume of ripe apples on to the still, hot air.

Baffled, she shifted her position slightly. Mr Turner's wiry figure stood between her and the boundary hedge and she now saw what she had not been able to see before. A small fruit ladder was propped up into the boughs of an apple tree whose boughs overhung Sarah and Alec's garden, but which was, unmistakably, Mr Turner's property. She had no idea of the legal position, but her anger wavered.

As if sensing a breach in the enemy's defences, Mr Turner spoke, chiming in with her thoughts. 'Them apples is mine.' He turned his head. 'All mine, them what overhang the hedge. No point in wasting them.'

Sarah's gaze followed his. Mr Turner's trees overhung their hedge all along this boundary and one comprehensive glance told her that he must have been busy here for days, whenever she was out of the way. All the trees, except the one at the far end, had been stripped. Yesterday she had been so engrossed in studying the hedge itself that she had failed to notice any of this, and she felt that she was, quite unfairly, rapidly losing ground. The old man, on the other hand, obviously beginning to feel that his position was, after all, defensible, was visibly reviving.

Suddenly the memory of all that she had suffered over the last few days filled her with a vast, searing anger. 'Mr Turner, you've been watching me, waiting until I was out to sneak over here and pick your apples.' It was a statement, not a question.

Beneath her accusatory gaze his eyes fell. 'No point in wasting them,' he muttered again. 'Not,' he said, rallying, 'like some folk.' And his eyes moved briefly, voraciously, over the laden trees in the garden. When he looked back at Sarah she saw there an unmistakable contempt for people such as herself who let good fruit hang on the trees until it dropped.

'What we do with our own fruit is our affair, not yours.' Briefly, amazement kept her silent. She would not have believed that she was capable of speaking to anyone with such acerbity. Then she realized that he had managed to slide away from the important issue and anger drove her on. 'That was you I saw peering at me on Monday, wasn't it? When I looked into your yard and saw you about to go into your caravan?' She took his silence for assent and, clenching her hands by her sides to stop them trembling, brought out the crucial question: 'Was it you who shut me in the shed, just afterwards?'

His head jerked upwards. 'Shut you in the shed?' This was something he could vehemently deny, and he seized the opportunity. Righteous indignation vibrated in every syllable. 'No, it was not. Why should I do that?'

Sarah shook her head. She felt hopelessly confused again. Only a moment ago it had all seemed crystal clear. She fastened on the one positive fact which seemed to have emerged. She must be sure about that. 'But you have been watching me?'

His minor victory seemed to have given the old man courage. 'Well, I have been keeping an eye on you, like, so I could – ' a gleam of inspiration illumined the small eyes – 'so I could pick my apples without . . . inconveniencing you,' he finished triumphantly.

Sarah was overcome by a vast weariness, brought about by deflation, disappointment, frustration and sheer hopelessness that anything constructive could be achieved by this conversation. She made one last effort. She had to know. 'And you haven't . . .' She had been going to ask if he had been responsible for the cards, but couldn't bring herself to do so. What was the point? He was nothing more than a mean, greedy, rather pathetic old man. She felt an overwhelming need to return to the sanctuary of the kitchen and try to assimilate the implications of this encounter. '. . . You didn't,' she amended hastily, 'think of simply asking our permission?'

This innocent question evoked a surprising response. His eyes dropped and he moved uneasily from one foot to the other.

'Why not? We wouldn't have minded in the least.' She couldn't understand his attitude until she caught a fleeting glance guiltily directed at the laden boughs above her head. Of course! He hadn't liked to ask

94

because of that rotten trick he had played upon them that first autumn. Unaccountably she felt a sudden access of sympathy for him. To have so little in his life that he should be prepared to go to these lengths just to reclaim a few boxes of apples indicated a barrenness which appalled her. She smiled and added gently, 'Next year you can do it without asking. We won't mind.'

Mr Turner looked at her incredulously. Like a schoolboy who expects a punishment and is let off when he least anticipates it, he decided to retreat before this happy state of affairs changed for the worse. He touched the brim of his ancient trilby. 'Thank you, Mrs Royd.' Picking up his apple box he headed for the gap in the hedge. He put it down, made his way through the opening in a crouching position and reappeared briefly to drag the box through behind him. Sarah was left standing alone in the orchard, the victor on the battlefield.

But she didn't feel victorious. She felt no triumph, no elation, merely a return of the overwhelming weariness of a few minutes before. Turning, she made her way unseeingly back across the orchard area, feet trailing through the grass, to the lawn, the terrace, the front door. In the kitchen she sat down heavily in the rocking chair and closed her eyes.

The incident had left her hopelessly confused, and she pressed her hands to her forehead, trying to disentangle her thoughts. It now seemed that two people, not one, had been responsible for the alarms of the last few days. Her sensation of being watched had, it seemed, emanated only partly from Mr Turner's surveillance. The whole business of the cards, the way they had been planted then, except for yesterday's, removed the figure she had seen on Sunday night; the incident when she had been shut in the shed; the footsteps she had heard in the house yesterday: none of these had been explained away.

Who could be responsible for them, and why? There had to be a reason, a motive behind them. Whom could she have antagonized to this extent? Action of this kind, so purposeful, so intensive, denoted a depth of malice which terrified her. However much she tried to reassure herself, the thought that anyone could hate her as much as this horrified her. How could she, she asked herself again, how could anyone commit against another person an offence sufficiently great to provoke this kind of action without being aware of it? It didn't seem possible that she could have, but she must have.

Surely, too, such deep, personal animosity could only be aroused in someone with whom one had a close relationship. And she had so few really close friends. Apart from Mary and Alec, she had never been sufficiently involved with anyone to have the power to hurt them.

She opened her eyes in shock. Suppose either Mary or Alec was responsible? No, it wasn't possible. She knew both of them too well; she would have known if she had ever really hurt either of them. She tried to think back. Her friendship with Mary went back a long way, but she could not remember ever having a serious quarrel with her, or of consciously doing anything to hurt her. Could she have done so without realizing it? If that were so, no amount of thinking would give her the answer. If she had been unaware of it at the time, she would be unlikely to find out now. And anyway, she thought conclusively, Mary couldn't have been in the garden on Monday morning when the second card had appeared and Sarah had been shut in the shed: she had been teaching. Monday, Wednesday and Thursday mornings, she had said.

But if she were capable of carrying out this vicious campaign against Sarah, she would be capable of lying about that. In her heart Sarah could not believe that her friend was capable of such coldly calculated venom, but she had to know. For her own peace of mind she had to be sure.

Feeling like Judas, Sarah went into the sitting-room, found the number in the directory, picked up the telephone and dialled the number of the school where Mary worked.

'Hullo? Is that Ridgeway Primary School? I'm sorry to bother you, but I wonder if you could help me. I had a coffee morning here at my house on Monday morning and somebody dropped a rather valuable brooch. I expected the owner to ring up and claim it, but she hasn't and I am trying to ring everyone who was here. I know I invited Mrs Godwin, who teaches at your school, but I can't remember if she came. I wonder if you could tell me whether or not she was teaching on Monday? If so, I can cross her off my list.' It wasn't very plausible, but it was the best she could do on the spur of the moment.

'Just one moment, please, and I'll check.'

Sarah waited tensely, her hands slippery on the receiver. What if the answer should be no, she wasn't here on Monday? But it wouldn't be. It couldn't be. Nausea gripped her and she swallowed several times in rapid succession to ward it off.

'Hullo? I'm afraid the brooch couldn't belong to Mrs Godwin. She was definitely here on Monday morning. In fact, as I was checking the timetable I distinctly remembered seeing her here myself.'

'Thank you very much.' Sarah's voice came out as a croak, and she replaced the receiver gently, overwhelmed by relief and guilt. How could she have doubted Mary? She made her way into the kitchen and sank once more into her chair.

And Alec? It was unthinkable that it could be he who was torturing her like this, but she made herself contemplate the possibility. He was a proud man. Could the concession he had been forced to make over the house have affected him more deeply than she had thought? She remembered how, only this morning, she had been thinking how surprising it was that he had never referred to it again after he had given in, not even in an argument, when stored-up bitterness has a way of erupting unexpectedly.

She stood up impatiently. She was letting her fear affect her judgement. She began to pace restlessly up and down the kitchen. Alec was not a vindictive man, one who held a grudge. If he had been, she could not have failed to see it during the years she had known him. It would have become obvious at some time, directed against someone. And she had seen no trace of it.

She came to rest by the kitchen sink and gazed abstractedly out of the window, hands resting lightly on the cold, steel surface. Against her will her thoughts moved relentlessly on. He could, nevertheless, have planted that first card in her handbag. Who better placed than he to do so? And he had had ample opportunity to remove it from the beam over the fireplace. He could not, on the other hand, have been the man watching the house through binoculars, nor the figure on the lawn on Sunday night. Unless he had an accomplice?

She was suddenly possessed by a feeling of complete unreality. How had she come to be standing here by her familiar kitchen sink, thinking these wild, bizarre thoughts about her husband? The fear that she was losing her reason, that she was being tipped over the edge into insanity, clutched at her. Of course Alec couldn't be responsible. He loved her. He was selfish, often irritable and impatient, it was true, but she knew he loved her, needed her dependence on him to make him whole.

And so, once again, she was faced with the two

unanswerable questions. Who? And why? The doorbell rang and she went to answer it, thankful for the respite.

'Couldn't find a thing, Mrs Royd.' Bill Mudge was smiling sheepishly.

Sarah could see that it hurt his professional pride to admit defeat. 'Well, if you can't find it, I'm sure no one could.'

He shrugged. 'There it is. Can't be anything serious, at any rate. One day I'll catch her at it, then we'll see.' He shot a glance of affectionate exasperation at Sarah's car, standing smugly in the drive. 'I left the keys in the ignition. Shall I put it into the garage for you?'

'No, that's all right, Bill, I'll do it. I've got to get my shopping out of it. Thank you for bringing it back.'

She watched him cross the drive to the front gate, where Mick sat waiting in Bill's battered van, then went across to her own car. She might as well put it away now, then she would have some lunch. She glanced at her watch. Two o'clock already. She hadn't realized how late it was. She became aware that she was feeling distinctly hungry.

She drove into the garage and leaned over to pick up the two or three parcels which she had left on the passenger seat. As she picked up the last one she froze into immobility. Underneath it was a small white card, gleaming in the half-light of the garage. She had a sudden impulse to leave it there, get out of the car and pretend that it didn't exist, but even as she put out her hand to open the door of the car she knew that she couldn't do it. The compulsion to know what was written on it was too strong.

Unable to take her eyes from the small square of pasteboard, throat suddenly dry and heart thudding, she put out her hand to pick it up. The decision to look at it taken, she snatched at it in her haste and with fingers which had begun to shake she held it up before her, straining to see what the message was in the dim light.

There was no window in the garage and she realized at once that she could not decipher what was written on it. With an exclamation of annoyance she got out of the car and went to the door of the garage, peering at it as she went. The letters clarified and grouped themselves into recognizable shapes:

WE HAVE MADE A COVENANT WITH DEATH, AND WITH HELL ARE WE AT AN AGREEMENT.

IS.XXV111.15.

Chapter Ten

For a long moment Sarah stood, suspended in time, staring at the printed capitals in frozen disbelief. Then came the fear, sweeping over her, consuming her in its intensity. Without realizing what she was doing, she hurried, hands pressed to her swollen belly, through the open front door into the house. She shut and locked the door behind her and stood leaning against it for a moment before, with the blind instinct of the wounded animal seeking its lair, she tottered into the kitchen and sank into the rocking chair. After a moment she got up and locked the kitchen door, and checked that the french windows in the sitting-room were locked before collapsing again into the chair. She pressed her back into its cushions, her head against the cane-work, as if the comforting familiarity of it could give her the reassurance she so desperately needed.

Gradually her breathing steadied, the thumping of her heart subsided and she began to feel a little more in command of herself. Unwillingly she raised the card, which she still held clutched convulsively between fingers rigid with shock, and re-read the terrifying statement upon it. A statement which was both a statement and a promise. Slowly her mind began to work again.

This time, however, she felt an urgency which she had never felt before. This was the most direct threat she had received and held far more terrifying implications than any of the others. She could not allow herself to think 'He is going to kill me', but the unformulated thought was there and the need for action, any action, drove her to her feet.

What could she do? Ring Alec? She could imagine his reaction if she rang him at work and delivered an hysterical tirade over the telephone. He had told her never to ring him at work except in an emergency. But this would surely qualify as an emergency? Impelled by her need she hurried into the sitting-room and picked up the receiver. She started to dial, hesitated, then pressed the cut-out button and stood torn by indecision. She certainly felt that it was an emergency, but would he? She imagined his voice, faintly mocking but with an edge of anger to it.

'Really, Sarah, I can't see what all the fuss is about. Nothing has changed, not really.'

'But it has, it has.' She heard her own voice screaming out the reply, shrill with fear.

'In what way? We know that someone is out to frighten you, and this afternoon we shall be seeing the police about it. You are quite safe in the house so long as you lock up properly. You have, haven't you?'

'Yes, of course, but . . .'

'Good. Now,' (recognizing the need to calm her down), 'come on, darling. Everything is going to be all right. I'll be home in a few hours.'

And she, realizing the futility of argument: 'Yes, Alec.'

The conversation played itself through in her head and stopped. She replaced the receiver and stood looking at the squat black instrument, reluctant to relinquish the idea that it could bring her the help she so sorely needed. She wanted not only protection but comfort, reassurance. She would ring Mary – that was it. What day was it? Wednesday? A completely irrelevant thought struck her. The dinner party . . . it was this evening. With all that had happened she had completely forgotten about it. Impatiently she pushed the thought aside. She couldn't be bothered with trivialities at the moment. It was Wednesday afternoon, that was the point, and Mary had said that she was in most afternoons.

She snatched at the receiver and started to dial again, praying as she did so that Mary would be there. She dared not contemplate the possibility of her being out. What would she do then? The dialling tone began and repeated itself monotonously. She *was* out. Sarah waited much longer than she normally would, but it was obviously pointless to hope any longer. With something like despair, she lowered the receiver and had almost replaced it on its rest when a tiny voice said, 'Hullo?'

Sarah snatched the receiver up again, just in time to prevent the connection from being broken. 'Hullo, Mary. It's Sarah. I thought you must be out.'

'No, I was in the bath. I'm dripping all over the carpet. Can you be quick?'

Urgency swept away the apologies she would normally have made. 'Mary, can I come and see you?'

'Yes, of course. When would you like to come?'

'Now.' The word shot out of her and she tried to soften its impact. 'If it wouldn't be very inconvenient, of course.'

'No, that would be fine.' But there was a reservation of some kind in Mary's voice.

'You're sure?'

'Yes, of course I'm sure. If it were inconvenient I'd say so, you know that.'

Sarah knew that very well, but the reservation was still there in Mary's voice; she could hear it. What could it be? Anyway, she wasn't going to argue. Mary would see her and that was enough. 'I'll be there in ten minutes.' Then, her most pressing need met, suddenly visualizing Mary standing in a pool of water wrapped in a towel: 'You'd better get back to your bath. You'll freeze to death. 'Bye.'

'See you shortly, then.'

Now that action was promised she felt calmer and methodically she checked again that the doors were locked and the windows securely fastened. Rummaging in her handbag for her car keys she had a moment's panic when she couldn't find them, before she remembered that she must have left them in the ignition after the shock of finding the card.

On the way to Mary's house, she thought about the hint of reservation she had sensed in Mary's voice. What did it mean? Perhaps it was simply irritation at having been dragged out of the bath? No, it couldn't be that. Reluctantly, for she did not want to acknowledge that Mary may not have wanted to see her this afternoon, that her own need may have made her ignore Mary's wishes in the matter, she admitted to herself that it had not been noticeable until she had said she wanted to see Mary at once.

Perhaps Mary had had other plans for this afternoon and was slightly irritated at having to defer them. Although Sarah had rarely seen her ruffled she would be less than human if she did not become annoyed occasionally. Sarah decided that she would apologize immediately, as soon as she arrived. She was sure that, when Mary saw the card, she would understand Sarah's urgency.

This time the house stood silent when Sarah arrived and after ringing the bell she had to wait several minutes before she heard footsteps coming down the stairs and Mary opened the door.

'Mary. It is good of you to see me straight away like this. I am sorry if I've ruined your plans for the afternoon.'

'Don't be silly. I didn't have any. I had a bonfire at

lunch-time after coming home from work and I was just washing away the smell of smoke when you rang.'

'I'm sorry about that, too.'

'Sarah, it's all right. Do stop apologizing.' She waited until they were both seated, then said encouragingly: 'Now, what's the matter?'

'I had another card.' She took it out of her bag and handed it to Mary without looking at it. She had no need to refresh her memory, the words were branded on her mind.

Mary read it in silence. 'Hmm. A covenant with death. Very dramatic.'

Sarah stared at her, dumbfounded.

'Well, whoever this person is,' continued Mary calmly, 'he is certainly doing his very best to terrify you. And succeeding, by the look of you,' she added, glancing sharply at Sarah.

Sarah found her voice. 'Is that all you have to say? I mean . . . you seem to be taking it very calmly.'

'Well, I see no point in giving this . . . person the satisfaction of seeing that he is achieving the desired effect.'

'But . . . but . . . don't you think this card is any worse than the others?'

'In what way?'

'Well . . . it's more of a direct threat.'

'I don't know. I don't feel there can be any real danger, otherwise something more direct would have happened by now. I think he's just enjoying a cat and mouse game. I should try not to let him see that he is succeeding in frightening you, if I were you.'

'But who can be doing it, Mary? And why?'

'I just don't know. Perhaps he picked you at random. But I feel certain somehow that it won't go beyond this sort of thing.' She tapped the card in her lap. 'Please, Sarah, do try not to get into such a state about it. It can't be doing the baby much good.'

105

'No, I know.'

'Everything's all right there, is it? No complications?'

'No, everything's fine.'

Mary leaned forward in her chair. 'Sarah, are you worrying about the baby?'

'Well, a bit, I suppose. Wondering if everything will be all right. I haven't thought about it so much over the last few days, I've been too worried about all this.'

'Why shouldn't it be all right?'

'I know . . . All the same . . .'

'Everyone worries at a time like this. It's perfectly natural. I certainly did.'

'Did you, really?' Sarah marvelled at the thought of Mary worrying about her pregnancy.

'Yes, of course I did. I had all kinds of terrifying thoughts. But Lucy was fine, just as your baby will be fine. Have you finally decided on names yet?'

'Yes, Ruth if it is a girl, Adrian if it's a boy.'

'Mmm. I like those.'

Sarah suddenly realized that the purpose of her visit had slipped away. 'Mary, I wondered . . . would you mind very much if I stayed here until about five? Alec should be home at about half-past, and then we're going to the police. It's all going to be rather a rush. I only remembered just before I came out that we're having dinner with Angela and Frank this evening.'

'Of course you can stay, if you want to . . . going to the police, you say?'

'Yes, we decided last night. Your telephone call helped a lot.'

Mary looked embarrassed. 'Well, I didn't know what to do. I don't like interfering, on principle. But you were in such a state that I decided to take the plunge. I hope you weren't too angry with me.'

'To be honest, I was at first. But it did help, so I ended up feeling grateful. Alec thinks you are a level-headed sort of person, so he took much more notice of what you said. And when I showed him the gap in the hedge I think he really was convinced – not that that is relevant, as it turns out.' She noticed that Mary was looking confused. 'Oh . . . of course, you haven't heard about that, have you?' And she launched into an account of how she had found the gap and how Alec had reacted. She ended with the story of her meeting with Mr Turner that morning. She couldn't help dramatizing it, and by the time she had finished they were both laughing.

'What a pathetic creature! Imagine going to all that trouble just to salvage a few boxes of apples! Anyway, it will save you a trip to the police station.'

Sarah stopped laughing abruptly. 'What do you mean?'

'Well, you won't need to go now, will you?'

'Why not?'

'From what you were saying, I gather it was the gap in the hedge which made Alec decide to take action. Now that that is explained away, perhaps he will change his mind.'

'But it wasn't only that!' cried Sarah. 'Until last night he hadn't heard about what happened on Monday – when I was shut in the shed. And until last night he just hadn't been disposed to listen. Did I tell you the Hannery Collection came in on Friday?'

Mary shook her head.

'Well, that's the point. You know how much he's been looking forward to its arrival, and the minute it arrived there I was, completely immersed in my own problems, just when he had been looking forward to telling me all about it. Naturally he was hurt, and angry with me. Then you rang him yesterday, and although I was a bit cross with you at first for interfering, I was relieved really, because by the time he got home he was ready to listen to me. The gap in the hedge merely clinched things. So I don't think he'll change his mind now.'

'I don't know. I should think that, when he hears what you have just told me about Mr Turner, he might well reconsider. And you know Alec. If he makes up his mind that there is not enough evidence to go to the police, nothing would make him go.'

'But he already has made up his mind.' Sarah was exasperated. 'It's all arranged. We're going when he gets home from work.'

Mary made no reply, but merely sat gazing abstractedly down at her hands, which were loosely folded in her lap.

If only I could be as calm as that, thought Sarah in despair. But then, it's all very well for her to be calm; she is not the one who is threatened. She opened her mouth to say so, then closed it again. What was the point? Mary had the inflexible air of someone who had made up her mind. She doesn't believe me any more, thought Sarah suddenly. She is trying to hide it, but she doesn't believe me. She doesn't think Alec will go to the police, because she doesn't think it necessary, so she can't see why he should.

'Mary, why have you changed your mind?'

'About what?'

Sarah's courage failed her. She simply couldn't ask Mary why she had changed her mind about believing her, because she was afraid of what the answer would be. 'About going to the police.'

'Well . . . I suppose because I've had time to think about it, and I've decided that yesterday I was so upset by the state you were in that I didn't think properly before I made the suggestion.'

'Ah, I wondered when you would remember that it was your suggestion.'

'Sarah, don't be angry. Of course I remember. I've just had second thoughts about it, that's all.'

'But what has changed? I don't understand. After all, you didn't even know about the gap in the hedge when I saw you yesterday, so what I have just told you about Mr Turner shouldn't make any difference. There is no reason whatsoever for you to have changed your mind, so far as I can see.'

'I told you. I just think perhaps I was hustled into a wrong conclusion, that's all.'

'So I hustled you, did I?'

'Well, perhaps that was a bad word to choo . . .'

'You chose it,' snapped Sarah. She struggled to her feet. 'I can see there's no point in staying here.'

'Please, Sarah, don't go like this. Don't be upset.'

'What do you expect me to be?' said Sarah in a rare burst of temper. 'I came here expecting comfort and reassurance and find you back-pedalling as fast as you can. You just don't believe me any more, do you? You needn't try to hide it any more. Do you think I'm blind?'

'That's not true. Please, Sarah . . .' Mary, too, had risen and now gripped her arm fiercely.

'Oh, leave me alone!' Sarah could bear it no longer. She struck Mary's hand away from her arm and stumbled towards the door. One part of her longed to stay and be comforted, another part of her longed to get away, anywhere, and lick her wounds. For the moment the second need was the stronger and it drove her out of the house and into her car without looking back.

She sat for a moment composing herself. Careful now, she told herself. It's dangerous to drive like this. Wait a few minutes until you've calmed down. She sat, gripping the steering wheel and breathing deeply and evenly until she felt sufficiently composed to drive. She would go slowly and carefully and concentrate completely on her driving.

She had started the car before she realized that she didn't want to go home yet. Neither could she sit there

109

any longer, in front of Mary's house. Mary would think she was deliberately lingering in the hope that she would come out. She put the car into gear and drove out of the cul-de-sac and out of sight round the corner, where she stopped again for a few minutes to think. Where could she go? Somewhere where there were other people, where she would feel safe. The swimming baths. That was it. There she would be able to sit quietly for a while and think. She started the engine again and set off, frowning with concentration.

Emerging into the spectators' gallery at the baths, she was relieved to see that she was its sole occupant. At this time of day there was a lull between the groups of school children and the after-tea rush of older children and adults. There were, however, as Sarah had expected, a number of mothers with toddlers in the shallow pool. Mr Rogers had told her that more and more women seemed to be realizing the benefits of getting their children accustomed to the water early in life, and this was one of their favourite times to bring them. She noted with relief that he was not on duty this afternoon. He would have been surprised to see her here at this time of day, and as a spectator.

She sank on to a bench and closed her eyes. The interval, together with the tight control she had imposed on herself while driving, had taken much of the heat from the emotion she had felt on leaving Mary's house. But there was inside her an emptiness she had never felt before. Mary had always been there, utterly reliable. Although they were the same age, she had almost been the mother Sarah had never really had in the solace she had given her at times. Only Mary's presence had made boarding school tolerable, and after they had left school they had never lost touch. They had both been delighted when, four years before, Sarah and Alec had found the cottage only a few miles from Mary and David's new house.

In all the years, this was the first real rift between them. At a time when Sarah needed her perhaps more than she had ever needed her before, Mary had let her down. And it was not only pain but bewilderment which gripped her as she sat on her hard wooden bench, gazing unseeingly at the splashing figures far below, surrounded by the hollow, water-reflected echoes. Why? Why had Mary changed her mind overnight? Why was her attitude so different? Yesterday she had been full of concern – so full of concern that she had even taken the unprecedented step of ringing Alec to tell him so. She had urged Sarah to go to the police, to take it all seriously. Yet today she had shrugged it all off as an unpleasant practical joke, had suggested that her reaction yesterday had been rash and over-emotional, and had gone back on her suggestion that Sarah should go to the police. Surely there must be some other explanation for such a drastic change. But what?

Eventually, like someone emerging from a trance, Sarah sighed deeply; her eyes, until this moment turned inwards upon her thoughts, began to focus. There was not really any point in sitting here any longer. The more she thought about it the more bewildering it became. Inconsistency was not, and never had been, one of Mary's characteristics, and Sarah didn't see how this change of attitude could ever become comprehensible. She became aware that the pool was deserted now and that the attendant was shooting puzzled glances in her direction. She realized to her astonishment that the clock at the far end of the building showed five-fifteen. If she didn't leave at once Alec would be home before her. And it would all be rather a rush, with the visit to the police followed by the dinner party. She remembered with dismay that Mary and David would be there. How would she face Mary, in the circumstances, with a number of other people present?

111

She shook her head impatiently as she made her way carefully along between the narrow benches. She would worry about that later. Now she must concentrate on getting home, and on remembering all the details she must give to the police. On the way home she rehearsed them and gradually became aware of a mounting tension. And of something else, too, which she took several minutes to identify as acute hunger. Of course, she had been about to have some lunch when she had found the card and had gone shooting off to Mary's house. She must snatch something to eat before she and Alec left for the police station. Suddenly the prospect of taking positive action against her persecutor made her spirits rise. What a relief it would be, to hand the whole matter over to someone who would do something about it! She had had enough of talk, of speculation. The little car leapt forward as her foot went down hard upon the accelerator.

Chapter Eleven

She was in the kitchen biting into a ham sandwich when Alec arrived home, a few minutes after her.

'How's my starving wife?'

'Hungry. I didn't have any lunch.'

'Why ever not?'

'I'll explain on the way,' she said.

'On the way?'

'To the police station.'

A curious expression crept over Alec's face.

Sarah stopped eating. 'We are going, aren't we?'

Alec shook his head. 'I've been thinking. Perhaps . . .'

Sarah put down the sandwich on the plate carefully. 'Don't tell me. I've heard it all before. You've been thinking it over. We're taking it all too seriously. You don't think we ought to do anything about it. Not – ' her voice rose to a scream – 'not until it's too late, and I'm dead!' And she snatched up her handbag – rummaged frantically inside and flung the card furiously on to the table.

Alec made no move to pick it up. 'What do you mean – you've heard it all before?'

'From Mary. I went to see her after finding that – ' her finger stabbed angrily in the direction of the card – 'and I had as much comfort from her as I'm having from you.' Her anger dissolved abruptly into self-pity and, sitting down on the nearest chair, she burst into tears.

Alec was at her side at once, squatting down beside her. 'Sarah, don't cry, please don't cry. I can't bear to see you like this. Please stop. Darling, I do love you.' His arms around her hunched shoulders, he continued to soothe and pacify her, and gradually her sobs diminished, her tears abated. Alec released one arm to fish out his handkerchief. 'Here, blow.'

Obediently she did so and he smiled encouragingly at her. 'That's better.'

Sarah twisted the handkerchief miserably in her lap. She remembered how Alec had wanted to go to the police the night before. She should, she thought despairingly, have taken the chance when it was offered to her. By now she would have been feeling safe, secure in the knowledge that they were on the alert, aware of all that had happened. Now, she felt more alone than ever. Why, why had Alec changed his mind? It was completely incomprehensible. She had to know. 'Alec, why have you changed your mind?' She sucked in her breath and held it, afraid of the answer.

'I haven't changed my mind, at least, not exactly. I've just thought of a better way of dealing with it, that's all.'

Slowly Sarah released the air from her lungs, feeling the tension draining out of her with it. 'You mean, you still believe me? You don't think I'm making it all up?'

'Of course I believe you.' Alec's voice was unwontedly gentle and his sincerity beyond doubt.

Sarah felt weak with relief. 'I thought, when you said – or indicated,' she corrected herself, 'we weren't going to the police, that it meant you'd changed your mind about believing me.'

'You didn't give me a chance to say anything.' Alec's tone was dry. 'You took off like a rocket.'

'Darling, I'm sorry. It's just that I had such an awful row with Mary this afternoon.'

Alec's eyebrows shot up. 'A row with Mary?'

Sarah nodded miserably. 'She didn't believe me either. I mean,' she amended, seeing the ominous look on Alec's face, 'she didn't believe me, and I assumed therefore that you must have changed your mind about going to the police because you didn't believe me any more. That was the reason why I got upset so quickly.'

'Did she say she didn't believe you?'

Sarah thought hard. 'No,' she admitted reluctantly, 'she didn't. I just felt she didn't. You see, she suggested going to the police yesterday, then today she went back on the idea. Just as you have.' She could not prevent herself from sounding accusing.

'But, darling, I've just explained to you that, although I may have changed my mind about going to the police, it hasn't altered the fact that I believe all you have told me.'

There was no need for him to continue. It was unnecessary to state the obvious. If she had jumped to the wrong conclusion with Alec, could she have done the same with Mary? Had that awful row been over nothing? Had it been caused solely by herself, by the ideas she had wrongly attributed to Mary, by her own frustration and fear? What was the matter with her these days? She didn't usually behave like this, almost going out of her way to provoke arguments, dissolving into floods of tears at the slightest set-back, flying off the handle with scarcely any provocation.

'I don't know what's the matter with me these days.'

'Let's just say you're a little on edge, shall we?' Alec grinned at the understatement, inviting her to join in the joke.

She managed a faint, shame-faced smile. 'Alec, what did you mean when you said you'd thought of a better way of dealing with the problem?'

Alec stood up abruptly. 'I was afraid you'd ask me that.' He stretched his legs, cramped from the crouching position he had maintained for some time, and rubbed his thighs. 'I must be getting old.'

'Afraid I'd ask you? Why?'

'Because I don't want to tell you, not at the moment, anyway.'

'Why not?'

'I can't tell you that without giving it away, and I want to see if it works, first.'

'But I'd feel so much better if I knew that something was being done.'

'I told you. Something is being done.' He stooped, took her hands and pulled her gently to her feet. 'Please, darling, trust me, will you?'

Sarah hesitated. She was still dissatisfied, unwilling to let the matter rest.

'Come on, darling. Have I ever let you down?'

'Well, no, but . . .'

'Well, there you are then. Darling, you must believe me when I say that it is as important to me as it is to you to get this business sorted out. Can't we leave it there for the moment?'

Sarah was still reluctant. But at least she had Alec's support. He believed her, that was the important thing. 'All right, but will you promise that if your way doesn't work, we'll go to the police at the week-end?' She could see he hesitated. 'Please, Alec,' she pleaded. 'I don't think I can go on any longer than that. If as long. But I'll try, if you promise.'

'Very well. If nothing is resolved by Saturday, we'll go. I promise,' he added hastily, seeing the request shaping itself on Sarah's lips. He picked up the card from where it still lay on the table and read its message. His mouth tightened. 'I'll take this.' And he put it in his pocket.

The action reassured Sarah. Alec, it said, was now

in control. It was wonderfully relaxing after the insecurity and alarms of the last few days, to know that he had taken over the responsibility for action. She would have preferred to know exactly what he intended to do, of course, but at the moment she was prepared to settle for this. Saturday was, after all, only two days away. She would be very careful, stay out as much as possible, in places where there were plenty of people. She could see that, as far as Alec was concerned, the matter was for the moment closed, and nothing would be gained by pursuing it.

As she became once more aware of her surroundings, her eye fell on the clock. She was astounded to see that it was already twenty to seven. 'Alec, look, at the time! We're due at Angela's at a quarter to eight!'

'You're sure you feel up to going out?' His solicitude warmed her.

'Yes, I'm fine. I'm quite looking forward to it.'

'Well, if you want a bath you'd better go and have it.' He glanced at the half-eaten sandwich on the table. 'At least you should do justice to dinner.'

Sarah laughed as she went out. 'I certainly will.'

She had astonished herself by her statement that she was looking forward to the evening ahead, but as she went upstairs she found it was true. It was some time since they had been out to dinner and she was, in any case, eager to see how her new understanding of Angela would affect the relationship between them, uneasy for so long.

She and Angela had met at the Commercial College where Sarah had gone after leaving school. Neither of her parents had thought it very important that she should have a career, seeming to take it for granted that she would soon get married, and she had drifted into the Secretarial section for want of a better alternative. To her astonishment, she found that she had really enjoyed the course, and she had never regretted taking

117

it because it was through the work for which it qualified her that, later on, she had met Alec. She had filled in as a temporary replacement in the clerical department of the Archives Office in which he worked, and meeting him had transformed her life in a way she would never have believed possible.

Here, at last, was someone who wanted her for herself, to whom she was, apparently, indispensable. He had become the sun around which she revolved, the centre of her universe. Her gratitude towards him for loving her, for making her feel worthwhile at last, gave her a constant desire to please him, to make him happy. It was rare indeed for her to persist in disagreeing with him over anything. To provoke Alec's displeasure, constantly to be at loggerheads with him, was to live in a nightmare. This was why she would not, could not, go against his wishes and take her problem to the police without his agreement; why she was ready, now, to give in to his request that she should leave him to deal with the matter in his own way. As long as he was behind her, that was all that mattered.

As she lowered herself into the steaming, fragrant water she speculated on the action he intended to take. Perhaps he had hired a private detective? Or a body-guard? She visualized herself being followed at a distance of three paces by a massive individual with bulging muscles and threatening mien. She smiled to herself. As usual she was letting her imagination run away with her. She decided that speculation was pointless. She would just have to do as Alec had asked, and trust him to do whatever he thought best. He had been unusually gentle and understanding this evening.

How full of contradictions people were! Who would believe, seeing Alec as he had been this evening, that he was frequently as impatient, irritable and short-tempered as he had been that evening when she had shown him the first card. And look at herself, usually so quiet, complacent, meek, suddenly turned into a quarrelsome, hysterical virago!

What about Angela? What was she really like? Was she, as Alec thought, unsure of herself and desperately unhappy beneath that calm and elegant exterior? At the College she had stood out from the rest of the girls like a gold coin amongst a pile of copper ones. She had the kind of beauty which would stand out anywhere. Her long, thick glossy hair was that deep blue-black colour which Sarah had always thought was the most beautiful colour that hair could be; her skin was pale, and had a pearl-like sheen of translucency upon it which was nothing to do with make-up; dark blue eyes, black winged brows and a perfect figure completed the catalogue of Angela's perfections.

Unconsciously Sarah sighed. It had always seemed so unfair that Angela should have all these things and Sarah none. With looks like these it would have been understandable if Angela had been treated warily by the girls at the College, and it was a measure of her kind and unassuming nature that she had been one of the most popular. Her attainments in shorthand and typing had been ignored by her fellow students as irrelevant. Everyone took it for granted that as soon as Angela launched herself upon her 'career', some wealthy, eligible male would snap her up. Which he had.

It had all been almost boringly predictable. Angela had gone straight into Frank's firm from College. He had been every secretary's wealthy, eligible and good-looking dream. He had taken one look at Angela and fallen heavily. Unaccountably, Sarah had thought, his proposal had taken rather longer to come than she had expected. Wiggling her toes in the rapidly cooling water, she acknowledged now, looking back, that it was probably because Angela had refused to go to bed with him that he had finally proposed to her. For, there was no doubt about it, Frank was the world's worst womanizer, and must have hesitated before committing himself to one woman for life, even one as beautiful as Angela. And it wasn't long after they were married that he reverted to his normal behaviour. It seemed that he simply could not resist trying to win over every woman he met to an appreciation of his charm. Quite often that was all it amounted to, but his life was nevertheless sprinkled liberally with more serious affairs, and what hell that must be to live with, thought Sarah again, preparing to make the effort to heave herself out of the bath.

Usually she didn't spend long in front of the mirror, but tonight she paused for a moment to admire her dress, which she loved. She'd only worn it once before, but she knew it was absolutely right for her, and it gave her a rare self-confidence. It was made of pink, pleated chiffon, a deep vibrant pink which had exactly the right depth of colour to make her hair appear a richer brown than it was and bring a little reflected colour to her cheeks. High to the neck, it fitted snugly over the breast, a multitude of fine pleats falling to the ground from a seam just below them, blurring the outline of her swollen stomach. Except for the sleeves, the whole dress was firmly lined in a heavier material of the same colour as the chiffon, but the sleeves were transparent and very full, gathered into wide cuffs. It had cost far more than Sarah had been able to afford. Persuaded into trying it on by an insistent sales-girl, astonished at the transformed Sarah who had appeared in the mirror, she had bought it on impulse and awaited Alec's verdict with trepidation. His whole-hearted approval and admiration had prevented her from feeling guilty at her extravagance, and it was easily her favourite dress. And, she reflected as she ran the deliciously soft, fine, cobwebby material through her fingers, the style was a fashionable one; she would be able to wear it after the baby was born. She couldn't imagine that she would ever tire of it.

'Delicious,' said a voice behind her. 'I could eat you.' And Alec put his arms around her, and kissed the nape of her neck.

Sarah glowed. 'Are you nearly ready? Time's getting on.'

'If you could just tie my tie . . .'

And it was with a delightful sense of anticipation that, ten minutes later, they set off.

Chapter Twelve

For Sarah, to feel gay and light-hearted again was a miracle. The threats still lurked, of course, in the hidden recesses of her mind, but for the moment she was content that, in some mysterious way, she was able to put them aside, ignore them, pretend they did not exist. She was simply a young married woman in a pretty dress, about to give birth to her first, longed-for baby, on her way to a pleasant evening with friends, where civilized conversation would be spiced with the added enjoyment of excellent food and wine.

A tuneless drone emanating from Alec as he drove indicated that he, too, was in unusually high spirits. Sarah sat wrapped in a cocoon of pleasant anticipation, watching the dim shapes of trees and hedgerows materialize in the glare of the headlights and flash by, to be swallowed up in the darkness which closed behind them.

Angela and Frank lived in a beautiful Georgian house, an exceptionally fine example of that period when perfect proportions, perfect harmony of windows, doors, roof and chimney stacks were the criteria by which a house was judged. Built of mellow red brick with crisp white paintwork and an immaculately tended setting of velvety lawns and glowing flower-beds, it always reminded Sarah of a child's drawing: front door in the centre, two windows to the right, two windows to the left, five windows on the first floor, chimney-stack at each end.

As they turned into the drive the house, with welcoming lights streaming from many of its windows, conjured up images of elegant gatherings of powdered and bewigged gentlemen resplendent in satins and brocades, and gracious women exquisite in lace and crinolines, hair piled into incredible heights, fans coyly half revealing faces brilliant with rouge.

'If only one could see into the past of a house like that!' Alec chimed in with her thoughts. 'One day I must do a bit of research on it. It would be interesting to know its history.'

'I'd like to know more about the people who lived in it,' murmured Sarah, her imagination still peopled with dazzling figures from the past.

'And there's the difference between us. The practical and romantic approaches.' He parked the car neatly next to Mary and David's battered Ford, looking somewhat inappropriate in its present setting. 'I like facts, dates, lists, inventories; you like to imagine what the people felt who used them, how they behaved, and why.' He got out of the car and walked round to the passenger side to help Sarah out. 'But I wouldn't have you otherwise. Just imagine how dull life would be if we were both as prosaic as I am!'

Sarah laughed. 'I don't know. I often wish I had your capacity for seeing things clearly. I always seem to get bogged down in "ifs", "buts", and "perhapses".'

'Mutual admiration society,' said Alec as they mounted the two steps to the front door. And they were still smiling at each other as Angela opened the door, elegant as ever in a black dinner dress of soft crepe which discreetly displayed her lovely body, enhanced the ivory of her skin and accentuated the rich darkness of her hair, piled up this evening into a smooth, elaborate chignon. Sarah immediately felt dowdy, conscious of the clumsiness of her movements. She responded to Angela's greetings and followed her into the house with the inevitable feeling of gaucheness which Angela always seemed to induce in her.

While she waited in the spacious hall for Angela to return from showing Alec into the drawing-room, she glanced about her with the familiar mixture of pleasure and envy. The elegant proportions of all the rooms in this house had been enhanced by Angela's excellent taste, and by Frank's ability to supply the money to indulge it. The hall was wide, floored with large square black and white marble tiles, and the white-painted staircase rose up out of it in a graceful curve, its white carpet carefully avoiding the error of distracting the eye from its perfect proportions. And who but Angela, thought Sarah, as she thought each time she looked at this most impractical of floor coverings, who but Angela would put a white carpet on the stairs? Above a white-painted, panelled dado to waist-height on the staircase wall, the delicate sage-green silk wallpaper provided the perfect background for a number of oil paintings evenly disposed up its length. Originals, of course, thought Sarah cattily as she followed Angela's elegant rear-view up the luxurious expanse of carpet.

Angela and her home always combined to bring out the worst in her, she reflected sadly. Where were all her good resolutions now? Why was it that although aesthetically she derived great pleasure from the beauty which Angela had created about her, that pleasure was never unqualified? There always seemed to be some little twist of nastiness in her, as there had been just now, to prevent her from enjoying it without reservation.

And yet she felt no envy of Angela in the conventional sense. She did not envy her her house, her money or, heaven knew, her husband. As she trailed despondently behind Angela into the symphony of white and delicate greens that was her bedroom the answer suddenly came to her. What she envied was the assurance which was proclaimed in every carpet, every curtain, every piece of furniture, every lamp, picture, ornament. The house reflected Angela's sureness of taste as her own, in the dull safeness of its furnishings, reflected her uncertainty.

She took off her wrap and laid it on the bed beside Mary's shabby winter coat and became aware that Angela, who until now had been unusually quiet, was obviously waiting for an answer to the question which still trembled on the air, but which Sarah, in her preoccupation, had not heard.

'Sorry, Angela, what did you say?'

'How long is it now, until the baby is born?'

'It's due on November the twentieth. About three weeks.'

'You must be so excited.' Angela was smiling warmly, but her eyes, Sarah realized, were bleak.

Why, she's jealous of me, thought Sarah, astounded. Of the baby. Her conversation with Alec on the beach was suddenly vivid in her mind. Angela's childlessness, never mentioned between them, took on a different complexion. She had always assumed that Angela hadn't wanted children for purely selfish reasons, because she liked a good time and was not prepared to accept the limitations and responsibilities a baby would impose on her.

Now she realized how false that reasoning must be. It did not fit in with what she knew of Angela's nature, her warmth, her generosity. She saw now that Angela probably dared not risk having a baby for fear she might lose Frank in the process. For months she would lose her figure, her mobility, her availability, and then after the baby was born she would have to consider its needs first. And it would be fatal to leave Frank to his own devices for long. For the first time Sarah really

125

felt that, as Alec had said, Angela was not to be envied but pitied. She had been trapped by her beauty into a lifetime of uncertainty and emptiness.

Turning away towards the mirror of the dressing-table to hide the pity she knew must show in her eyes, Sarah tried frantically to think of something, anything which would diminish that bleakness in Angela's. 'Well, I am excited, of course, but,' she lied with inspiration, 'I've been meaning to ask you if, well . . . you might come and give me a bit of moral support sometimes.' She risked a quick glance at Angela's face mirrored before her and was rewarded by a glimmer of – what? – hope? – in it?

'How do you mean?'

'Well, you know me, always sure I'll make a mess of things. And babies are so tiny, aren't they? It frightens me, sometimes, to think of looking after it,' she lied valiantly. 'I wondered if you could come over from time to time and perhaps give me a hand. Though it seems a lot to ask.' She waited, holding her breath. Perhaps Angela might feel that the last thing she wanted was to help with someone else's baby. Perhaps she, Sarah, had only made things worse with her impulsive suggestion. She dared not look at Angela's face.

But she didn't have to wait for long. Almost before she had finished speaking Angela had cried, 'But I'd love to. I really would. This place runs itself, really, and I often have time on my hands.' Sarah had a sudden, vivid image of Angela wandering restlessly through the beautiful empty rooms which was replaced almost at once by one of herself and Angela sitting cosily on the rug in front of the (heavily guarded) fire in the sitting-room at home, playing with the baby. What had begun as a purely altruistic gesture, she realized, would have its satisfactions for her, too. She was suddenly angry with herself for all her past reservations about Angela. Angela's beauty, she saw now, had also denied her the satisfaction of having close women friends. Women were often wary, as she had been, of beauty in other women.

'Angela, look, I . . . I'm sorry if I've seemed stand-offish in the past.' It was immeasurably difficult to say, but having begun she was determined to go on and over-rode Angela's denials. 'Oh yes, I have, I know. It's just that I find it . . . difficult to be open with people, unreserved.'

Angela's face was transformed. 'Let's not talk about past misunderstandings. From now on, things will be different.' She tucked her arm into Sarah's as Sarah rose. 'We'd better go down now. The others will be wondering where we are.'

The drawing-room was full of warmth and light. The heavy apricot silk curtains had been drawn against the darkness, a small but cheerful fire burned in the grace-ful fireplace, and light from the apricot-shaded lamps was reflected back from creamy walls, tawny gold velvet and Angela's collection of coloured Victorian glass, set in illuminated arched alcoves on either side of the fireplace. The soft pile of the cream carpet sank luxuriously beneath Sarah's feet as she made her way across the room, Angela beside her.

Frank came to greet her with outstretched hands, dark hair immaculately groomed, brown eyes lighting up with self-conscious charm. 'Sarah, there you are! You look marvellous, doesn't she, darling?' As Angela smiled assent, the light kiss Frank planted on her cheek was a little more lingering than she would have wished, her hands, enfolded in his, received the bonus of a lightning caress from the tip of Frank's thumb against the soft, inner side of her wrist. As usual she had consciously to restrain herself from shrinking away a shade too quickly, from releasing her hands too abruptly. Over Frank's shoulder her eyes met those of

Alec, who was standing in front of the fire. The amused twinkle in them infuriated her.

David, too, advanced to meet her, his dry friendly peck on the cheek, square figure, untidy brown curly hair and benevolent brown eyes behind the spectacles a welcome contrast to Frank's suave elegance. Sarah gave him an affectionate smile, sat down beside Mary, demure in a cornflower blue dress which matched her eyes, and smiled radiantly at them all. She felt positively bursting with happiness. The only shadow over her pleasure was the memory of the quarrel with Mary, and she would seize the first opportunity of putting that right.

Her chance, however, did not come until after the delectable dinner of home-made vegetable soup, veal escalopes and French apple flan with cream. While Angela went to see to the coffee Sarah and Mary went upstairs to Angela's room and sat down together on the long padded stool in front of the dressing-table.

Sarah began at once. 'Mary, I am sorry about this afternoon.'

'There's no need to apologize, really.'

'But there is. I was thoroughly nasty to you. And after you had dropped everything to see me, too.'

'Nonsense, you were upset, that's all. And I didn't drop anything but my bath towel.'

Sarah couldn't raise the glimmer of an answering smile. 'Being upset was no excuse for the way I behaved.'

Mary clucked impatiently. 'Look, if it will make you any happier, I accept your apology. But I still don't think it necessary. Your behaviour was perfectly understandable, in the circumstances. And I really think that now you are going too far the other way, eating humble pie like this.'

'I realized later, when I thought about it, that I had jumped to conclusions too quickly. I thought, you see, that because you had changed your mind about the advisability of going to the police, it meant that you had changed your mind about the truth of what I had told you.' She waited, hopefully, for Mary's denials.

'You mean you thought that I thought you were making it all up? But why?'

Sarah shook her head miserably. 'I don't know. I suppose because I was afraid you might.'

'Well, I didn't think anything of the sort, so stop worrying about it. It was all a silly misunderstanding.' She took Sarah's hands and gave them a little shake. 'Come on now, cheer up. The others will be wondering what on earth I've done to you.'

'You two are looking very serious.'

Sarah and Mary both started. Neither of them had heard Angela's approach over the thick carpet, and had been too engrossed in their conversation to notice her reflection in the mirror. Mary smiled and patted Sarah's hands as she released them. 'I was just telling Sarah not to worry.'

Angela looked grave. 'Why, there's nothing wrong, is there?'

'No, of course not. Only you know what a worrier she is.'

'I certainly do. You should have seen her before her exams, at College!'

'I can imagine. She was bad enough at school.'

They both smiled indulgently at Sarah, who did her best to smile back. It was an effort, however. The brief conversation with Mary had brought the terrifying events of the last few days into the forefront of her mind again and the dark thoughts came flooding back, obscuring the faces of her companions, dimming the warmth and colour about her and revealing to her the impossibility of keeping them at bay for long.

'Are you all right, Sarah?' Mary's voice cut sharply into her despair. She must try to keep up a reasonably

129

convincing pretence of light-heartedness, for a little while longer at least. Then, as soon as she decently could, she would plead tiredness and Alec would take her home.

'Yes. Fine, thanks.' She gave the others no time to comment but went swiftly on: 'Are we all ready?' And she led the way downstairs.

They were comfortably ensconced in the drawing-room, sipping their coffee in a companionable silence when the dining-room door across the hall opened and a sudden burst of sound escaped from it. Raised voices and words such as 'disgrace', 'bigoted', 'clap-trap', floated across the hall. The women exchanged indulgent and quizzical looks. The three men often enjoyed what they called 'a good argument', but it rarely became as heated as this.

'I don't agree. I don't agree at all.' That was David. Sarah was surprised. He was the mildest of men and she could never recall his sounding so vehement before. She raised her eyebrows at Mary, who shrugged slightly.

'Well, I do.' This was Alec, equally positive. Again, Sarah was surprised. This meant that, whatever the argument was, Alec was siding with Frank against David, which she would not normally have expected to happen. Alec and David saw eye to eye on most things.

'There's far too much of this psychiatric nonsense these days.' Alec's voice grew louder as the men crossed the hall, and each word carried clearly through the half-open door of the drawing-room. ' "Poor little Jimmy," ' his voice mocked, ' "he couldn't help knocking the old lady on the head, he was very unhappy when he was a little boy and he thought she was his nasty old mother." It makes me furious. It's people like you, David, who encourage violence by being too soft with these characters. I'm all in favour of the old-fashioned deterrents, like Frank.' He stopped. By now all three men were inside the room and they grinned self-consciously at their wives.

'I'm afraid we got rather carried away,' apologized Alec.

'We're all dying to hear what you were arguing about,' smiled Angela forgivingly.

'Well . . .' The men all spoke together, and everyone burst out laughing.

'Come and sit down and have some coffee first.' Angela busied herself with cups and saucers, then, when all the men were served, sat back expectantly in her chair and said, 'Now, who's going to tell us?'

'We'll let David start, shall we, Alec?' Frank waved his hand in a gesture of generosity. 'As he's in the minority?'

Alec nodded assent.

David set his cup on a low table. 'We've been talking about that incident in the paper this morning. Involving that magistrate. Did you all see it?'

Mary and Angela nodded. Sarah, feeling foolish and ignorant, shook her head.

'Apparently last night a magistrate, I forget his name, answered a knock on his front door. There were two men outside, and when he opened the door they pushed their way inside and beat him up.' David paused. 'We were arguing about the sort of treatment or punishment the men ought to have. Frank and Alec think that a good whipping would teach them a sharp lesson, and would act as a deterrent to their ever doing anything similar again. I disagree. I think that they — or one of them anyway, the one who instigated the attack – should have psychiatric treatment.'

Sarah felt bewildered. 'I must be stupid, but I still don't see why you were all so worked up about it. After all, this argument is always cropping up, isn't it? You must have discussed it before.'

131

'Perhaps we haven't explained very clearly.' Alec put his cup down and leaned forward intently in his chair. 'This wasn't a run-of-the-mill assault case. The motive for the attack was that one of the men had been sent to prison for twelve months by this particular magistrate, and obviously felt he had been unjustly treated. According to the magistrate's wife, who saw the whole incident and was manhandled for trying to stop them, he kept on saying, "I didn't do it, you bastard. I didn't do it." And, just before he left, he shouted at her, "That'll teach him to think twice before he puts anyone else inside." Or something like that, anyway.'

There were nods of assent from the others.

'The point is, you see,' Alec went on pedantically, 'that behind this apparently trivial incident there is a vital principle at stake. This sort of action threatens the whole concept of justice as it is administered in this country. The law must be inviolate. We simply cannot afford to allow individuals to set themselves above it to execute private revenge. The result would inevitably be . . . Sarah?'

The word 'revenge' exploded in Sarah's head, echoing and re-echoing down the corridors of her mind. The room and its occupants started to spin round her, gently at first then faster, until with a final wild gyration, they were swallowed up in the merciful darkness.

The fiery sensation of brandy trickling down her throat stung her into consciousness. Someone was gently wiping her mouth. She opened her eyes. A circle of anxious faces surrounded her, with Alec closest, at the centre of it. Feebly she turned her head away from the teaspoon he was offering her again.

'I'm all right now.'

There was a general movement of relief and Frank and David tactfully withdrew to the other side of the room.

'Don't try to get up for a minute, darling. Just relax.'
Alec's face was grim, overlaid with relief.

'I must have fainted.' Sarah was overcome by embarrassment. 'What a stupid thing to do!'

'Don't be silly, Sarah. You make it sound like a matter of choice.' Angela's face was still full of concern. 'I thought you didn't look too well upstairs. You just lie there for a little while and then I think we ought to call your doctor. What do you think, Alec?'

Sarah shook her head feebly. 'No.'

'It might be a good idea, darling. After all, you don't usually go around fainting. You frightened us out of our wits.'

'I'm sorry.'

'Sarah, for heaven's sake.' The familiar note of exasperation was back. 'Stop apologizing. I was merely pointing out how concerned we are. I agree with Angela that we ought to call Doctor Blunsdon to have a look at you.' And a slight, almost imperceptible flicker of his eyes in Mary's direction called for support.

It came. 'I think so too, Sarah.'

'No. Really, I'm all right now.'

'All right, love.' Alec's voice was soothing, and his glance at the other two women said clearly, we'd better humour her. 'All the same,' he went on, 'I don't like it. Why should you faint, for no apparent reason? I don't think I can ever remember you fainting before.'

Yes, why did I? thought Sarah. Then, as if the knowledge had been waiting until she had recovered sufficiently to bear it, she remembered. Revenge, that was it. And she closed her eyes as all the implications came flooding back.

'Sarah?' There was urgency in Alec's voice. 'Sarah, are you all right?'

With an effort she opened her eyes and tried to sit up, automatically making an effort to distract Mary

133

and Alec from what they might see in them. They both knew her too well. Willing hands helped her.

Alec managed a faint, relieved smile. 'I thought you'd fainted again.'

Sarah conjured up a smile in return. 'No, I'm fine now, really. Just a bit tired.' She turned to Angela. 'I am sorry to be such a nuisance.'

'Not another word about it.'

Now that Sarah was sitting up, Frank approached again. 'Only too glad to see you looking better. Feel like a tot of brandy?'

Sarah shook her head. 'No thank you, Frank. I think that perhaps it might be sensible if I went home now.'

'I'll get your wrap.' Angela left swiftly and was back in a few moments.

They left amongst apologies on Sarah's part and expressions of concern on the part of everyone else, and it was with a sigh of relief that Sarah sank back into her seat in the car, leaving the others standing waving in a tight group on the portico, silhouetted against the brilliant light from the hall.

Chapter Thirteen

There was an uneasy silence as Alec drove down the drive and turned out on to the road. Sarah could not guess what he was thinking, and a quick glance at him revealed nothing. It was too dark in the car to see properly. She knew he would not be content to let the matter rest as it was, but hesitated to open the conversation as she did not know what his reaction would be when she told him the real reason why she had fainted. In any case, she wanted time to assimilate the implications of the blinding flash of understanding which had come upon her so suddenly and unexpectedly.

Now that she understood, it all seemed so simple. She really couldn't understand why she hadn't seen it before. Alec had even specified the motive behind the frightening events of the last few days, when they had been discussing them on – when was it? – last night. That was it. 'The classic revenge motif' he had called it. And she still hadn't seen, still hadn't understood.

The car slowed down as the headlights picked out a rabbit running frantically along the road ahead of them, seeking a way through the hedge to safety. With a final bob of its tail it was gone. The break in the even rhythm of the drive precipitated Alec into speech.

'You're very quiet.'

'I was thinking.'

'What about?'

'About that business with the magistrate.'

'What, exactly, about it?' Alec's tone was mild, betraying no more than normal interest, but his hands on the steering wheel, illuminated by the faint glow from the dashboard lights, were clenched tightly around it.

Her courage failed her. She felt confused, bewildered, not about this new idea, but about Alec. She didn't know what to expect of him any more. What, for example, was his real reason for changing his mind about going to the police? When he arrived home this evening nothing had changed from last night, when she had had difficulty in restraining him from doing so. What other action could he be taking? And why wouldn't he tell her what it was? It all seemed very vague, and dissatisfaction welled up in her. Perhaps when he heard this idea of hers he would change his mind. She opened her mouth to speak, then closed it again. No, before she told him, she wanted to think it out properly. Conscious that he was still awaiting an answer to his question, she cast frantically around in her mind for a suitable reply. Thankfully, she remembered that she had not yet told him about her encounter with Mr Turner this afternoon. That would distract him.

'Nothing much. I was just thinking about it. By the way, I forgot to tell you. The mystery of the gap in the hedge is solved.'

'Solved? How?'

'When I came home from relaxation class I had to leave the car at the garage so I walked home. I caught Mr Turner stripping all the apples off those branches of his trees which overhang our hedge.'

'I see.' Alec's tone was ominous. 'I shall have to have a word with Mr Turner.'

'Oh no, Alec.'

'Why not? He has absolutely no right to come into our garden like that.'

136

'But he is such a pathetic little man, Alec. All that trouble for a few boxes of apples. I . . . I told him that in future he could come in and pick them without asking.'

'You did what?' They were home. Alec swung the car into the drive and drove straight in through the open garage doors.

'Please, Alec, don't be angry. Just think how awful it would be to have so little in life that a couple of hundredweight of apples should mean so much to you.'

They got out of the car and walked in silence to the front door. Alec fumbled with his key, then preceded Sarah into the house, switching the lights on for her as he went. In the kitchen he turned to face her. 'That's all very well, but you've been frightened out of your wits by that "pathetic little man", as you call him, these last few days. You surely don't mean that we should ignore all that? I suppose he's been spying on you to see when you were out, and he was caught this morning because you came back without the car?'

Sarah nodded. 'Yes, but . . .'

'Well, there you are. We can't just let it go.'

'But, Alec, don't you see? That's not important.'

'What do you mean, not important?' Alec's face was incredulous. 'For days now every time I've come home you've been quivering like a jelly, frightened out of your wits. And you say that it's not important, and expect me to ignore it?'

'But it's not the spying that's been worrying me. At least, it has, but that's different.'

'What do you mean? You're not making sense!'

Sarah sank wearily into her rocking chair. 'I do wish you wouldn't shout. I can't think.'

Alec sat down on a chair beside her. 'All right, I'm sorry. Now, what do you mean?'

'There must,' said Sarah, slowly and carefully, as if reciting a lesson learned by heart, 'have been two

137

people watching me, Mr Turner and somebody else. No – ' as Alec opened his mouth to interrupt – 'please, Alec, let me finish. Mr Turner's activities explain the gap in the hedge, certainly, and no doubt it was he who was watching me from behind the washing-line. He could possibly, though I doubt it, have been the man watching the house through binoculars. But all the other things, the cards, the man watching the house on Sunday night, my being shut in the shed, the footsteps I heard in the house yesterday afternoon, all those are still unexplained.'

Alec was silent. He made a hopeless gesture with his hands.

'Alec, why did you change your mind about going to the police?'

'Sarah, love – ' there was something approaching despair in his voice – 'don't let's go into that all over again.'

'But I want to know. I know I promised to leave it until Saturday, but I can't just wait in the dark like this. Don't you see, if I understood, I wouldn't mind waiting so much? Last night you were urging me to see them at once, and if I hadn't been so tired we would have. I wish I had, now. Then, this afternoon, you had changed your mind. And I know you don't change your mind about anything without good reason. So what was the reason? Please tell me. Something must have happened to make you change it. What was it?' Her hand clutched at his sleeve as if the urgency of her grip would drag the information out of him.

Alec shook his head. Uncharacteristically, he seemed at a loss for words.

'Alec?'

He shook his head again. 'Leave it, Sarah, it's hopeless. We've discussed it all ways and we never get anywhere. And as I told you earlier, I am doing something about it. Please, let's leave it until Saturday, as we said we would.'

'But we can't leave it now. Not when I think I've found the answer.'

Alec's head came up with a jerk. 'What do you mean?'

'You gave it to me, really, last night, when we were talking about it. It was you who spotted it, the motive I mean. Revenge.'

'But I thought we decided there wasn't anyone who had any reason whatsoever for wishing to revenge himself upon you.'

'It wasn't until you were talking about that magistrate this evening that I realized that that might not be so. As I understood it, one of the men who attacked him held a grudge against him, because he felt he'd been wrongly convicted. Is that right?'

Alec nodded.

'Well then, suppose, just suppose, that someone had a grudge against my father. It would be a much more serious grudge because the offences my father heard would be more serious than those for which a magistrate can convict, and the punishment correspondingly more severe. Suppose this man were sent to prison for some years, and that all the while he was there he nursed this grudge. Then he hears my father is dead, but the grudge is so much part of him by then he cannot give it up. So he looks for another way of punishing my father, and the only way left is by punishing . . . me.' Her voice trailed away, its impetus lost.

'But, Sarah, that's fantastic, literally.' He shook his head wonderingly, clearly incredulous that she could have thought up anything so wildly improbable.

'Why is it fantastic? I don't see it at all. It is merely carrying that incident with the magistrate one step further. And, surely, the longer a grudge is nursed, the more bitter it grows. And there could be all sorts of other things to feed it. Maybe while he was in prison his wife deserted him. That happens quite frequently, I believe. And he would blame that on my father too.' Her voice rose in an effort to convince him. 'Don't you see?'

'Of course I see the logic of what you are saying.' He took her hand gently in his. 'But I'm not sure if you are letting your imagination run away with you. You are feeling overwrought and anxious about the baby, and this is making you liable to grasp at any solution, however improbable.'

Sarah took her hands impatiently away from his. 'That has nothing to do with it.'

'So that was why you fainted this evening, because this solution suddenly came to you.'

'Yes. It was such a shock, you see, when I understood.'

'Darling, I do wish you would go and see Doctor Blunsdon.'

'And I wish you would stop saying that. There's nothing the matter with me. I told you, I'm perfectly all right. I'm due to go to the clinic again on Friday morning anyway. If only, if only this wretched business could be cleared up, I wouldn't have a care in the world.'

Alec stood up. 'Let's sleep on it. Come on, you look exhausted. Nothing is going to happen before morning.' He put out his hand and pulled her gently to her feet.

Sarah made no resistance, but as she started wearily up the stairs, holding on to the hand-rail they had fixed into the wall for support, she felt full of despair. Nothing had been resolved, nothing decided, Alec had brushed aside her solution and she felt more confused than ever. She still couldn't see why he would not explain his reason for not going to the police, or for refusing to tell her what plan of action he had in mind. Her feet came to a halt half-way up the stairs as she realized there could only be one explanation for his behaviour. Alec must believe that telling her would hurt her more than not telling her.

The stairs ahead of her suddenly seemed too steep to climb, the future too frightening to contemplate.

'Tired, love?' Alec's arm was firm around her waist as he caught her up. 'Come on, up we go.'

As if I were a child, she thought resentfully. But unresistingly she allowed herself to be supported upstairs along the landing and into the bedroom.

In bed she felt as though she were separated from Alec by a great gulf instead of by a few inches of bed. She had never felt so frightened, nor so alone before. Cut off from Alec and from Mary by an incomprehensible barrier, she felt that each day the alien presence of the watcher was coming closer to her and becoming more threatening.

Eventually self-pity drove out every other feeling and she wept, silently, the tears sliding down her face and soaking into the pillow behind her ears. The rhythm of Alec's steady breathing did not alter. He was obviously sound asleep, and with this final abandonment she turned over on to her side, clasped the pillow desperately to her face, and gave herself up to grief.

Chapter Fourteen

Sarah awoke to the sound of the curtains being drawn, and a delicious smell of coffee.

'Breakfast.' Alec leaned over her, smiling, and kissed her lightly on the forehead.

'What time is it?' She felt confused, heavy-eyed.

'Half-past eight.'

Dismayed, Sarah struggled into a sitting position. In their six years of marriage she had never before failed to get up and cook Alec's breakfast for him.

'I'm just leaving. I thought it would do you good to lie in for a while this morning.'

He had drawn a small table up to the bedside, and on it stood a breakfast tray: orange juice, a small pot of coffee, sugar, cream, a boiled egg topped with a scarlet and white egg cosy which Sarah had bought in a moment of weakness at a church sale of work, two thin slices of toast cooked crisply as she liked them, butter, marmalade, and a single yellow rose in a crystal holder, the whole arranged on a fair white cloth.

'Alec, how lovely! Thank you. I'm sorry I overslept.'

'Do you good. You obviously needed it. I must be off now. I'll be home at the usual time.'

'All right, darling. 'Bye.'

They kissed, briefly, and he was gone.

Left alone, Sarah looked at the carefully arranged breakfast tray. She drank the orange juice, then, smiling, took the ridiculous cosy off the egg. Underneath on the eggshell was printed 'I LOVE YOU.' Staring at it, she began to cry. If Alec loved her, why couldn't he see how desperately she needed to know what he was doing about the terrifying situation in which she found herself? What could be worse than living in this state of uncertainty?

Gradually her tears abated and she went to the bathroom and bathed her face in cold water. Her eyes looked red and puffy, her face pinched and pale. She really must try to pull herself together. She had no alternative. Somehow she must get through today and tomorrow, and then it would be Saturday. Her expression hardened. If, by Saturday, Alec had not come up with some kind of solution, she would go to the police without his approval, if necessary.

She looked incredulously at the determined grey eyes reflected in the mirror, the grim, compressed line of her lips. If anyone had told her, a few weeks ago, that she would make up her mind deliberately to go against Alec's wishes, she would not have believed him. What was happening to her? She thought back over the last few days. Although she had ultimately given in to Alec in every argument, she could never remember having so many arguments with him before. Usually she automatically deferred to his wishes. She had been so grateful to him for loving her that she would have done anything to please him.

She thought how, only last Saturday, she had finally abandoned her hopes of his being there when the baby was born. The only time she could ever remember having held out against him until she got her own way had been over the house and then, as now, the strength of her need had given her the courage to go against his wishes.

She got back into bed and, feeling an absurd reluctance to crack the eggshell and break up the carefully printed letters, nibbled at a piece of toast and drank some reviving black coffee.

What should she do today? She couldn't stay at home, that was certain. She remembered her resolution of the night before, to stay out as much as possible, in places where there were plenty of people. But what she needed was not merely an avoidance of danger but action, positive, constructive action, some way of testing the truth of her theory. But how? Lay a trap for the man? She shivered. That was out of the question. Apart from the fact that she simply did not have the courage to do such a thing, she could not risk endangering the baby. She folded her hands protectively over her stomach and for a moment gave herself up to the pleasure of savouring the movements she felt within her.

It was no good. She couldn't think of any way in which she could hit back at her unseen enemy. She was too vulnerable, because of the child. She would go to the sea for the day. She pushed aside the bedclothes, got out of bed and went across to the window. Another peaceful autumn morning greeted her, mist just lifting from the grass, sun just beginning to reach and light up the glowing bronze and gold of the chrysanthemums at the far side of the garden.

Downstairs she washed up the breakfast dishes, took some chops out of the freezer to defrost for supper, and went back upstairs to fetch a cardigan. She would stay out all day and not arrive home until Alec did. She would go to a busy seaside town, where she would be safe amongst other people. Automatically she checked that the upstairs windows were securely fastened. In the nursery she paused. Something was nudging at the edge of her consciousness. What was it? She looked around, puzzled. Everything stood just as usual, with its intolerable air of waiting to be brought to life. Pram, carricot, cot, chair, all mocking her with their emptiness. Her eyes moved on around the room. Cut-out figures on the wall, chest of drawers, toys sitting on it, bath, pile of junk, cupboard . . . pile of junk. Of course. The scrapbook. In a few joyous strides she crossed to where it lay, such a familiar sight as to be almost invisible by now, and picked it up.

This might give her the answer. There were many of her father's cases in it. Perhaps one of them might be the one she sought. With fingers that had begun to shake she started to leaf frantically through it. It was hopeless, of course. Such a task would take a long time, hours perhaps. But she couldn't bear to contemplate staying in the house all day. What she needed was somewhere quiet where she would be able to study it carefully, undisturbed. But somewhere safe, where there would be other people about her. She racked her brains, trying to think of such a place. The library, that was it. The County Students Library. It would be ideal. Quiet, safe, conducive to concentration.

Tucking the scrapbook under her arm, she completed the check of doors and windows, hunted out some sheets of paper and a pencil, picked up her handbag and left.

She passed the swimming baths with a qualm of guilt. Mr Rogers would be wondering where she was, thinking perhaps that she had gone into hospital to have the baby. It was the first time she had failed to go swimming on a Thursday for months. It was, she thought bitterly, a measure of the extent to which she had become preoccupied by this wretched business, that she had completely forgotten about her swimming session.

At the library she parked her car and walked eagerly towards the main entrance. It was a new building, and the pride of the County Council. Built in the shape of a scallop shell its graceful silhouette, hugging the top of a slight hill on the edge of the town, echoed the curves of the rising ground on which it stood and was visible for some distance around in all directions.

Inside, the lines of the scallop radiated from the librarians' curved counters in the form of book-lined bays, each equipped with tables, reading lamps and comfortable chairs.

Sarah settled down where she was clearly visible from the counters and laid the scrapbook on the table before her. She opened it eagerly and began to read. Perhaps at last she would find a weapon with which to fight her enemy.

The cuttings, she saw, spanned a period of sixteen years, beginning in 1953 with the brief announcement that her father had been made a Judge in the High Court, obviously cut from the Court Page of the *Morning Post*. She began to skim quickly through the pages, then checked herself. She must curb her eagerness. There was no short cut. She would have to read each cutting methodically and carefully, looking out especially for any hint of grievance on the part of any criminal and for any breath of bias on the part of her father which might have created such a feeling in the accused man.

One useful eliminating factor was that she could discount any case where the sentence must have been worked out years ago; presumably, if she were right about this, the man would hardly wait for any length of time after coming out of prison to carry out the retribution he had promised himself. So she must look for cases where the sentence would terminate about now.

She wrinkled her brow. She had forgotten about remission for good conduct. This varied so much that it would be very difficult to test her theory properly. At once a host of other doubts assailed her. Her father must have heard thousands of cases which were not sufficiently newsworthy to have been reported in the papers. And even if that particular case had been reported, the information she was seeking might not be given. There was also the possibility that the man might have given no hint of his feelings. He might have kept his intention of revenge a complete secret.

Sarah shook her head impatiently to dispel these gloomy forebodings. The scrapbook was her only hope. She would be as thorough as possible and pray that she might be fortunate enough to find something.

In a business-like manner she took a sheet of paper and drew three columns on it: one for the names of men who might have felt unjustly treated, one for the names of those who would be due to finish their prison sentences at about this time, and one for the names of men who did not fall into either category but whom she felt would be worth investigating. What she would really like to find, of course, would be a man who fitted into both of the first two columns, but she felt that it would be too good to be true if she found one. She began to read with complete concentration, determined to miss nothing of significance.

The cuttings held reports long and short, detailed and sketchy, dull and sensational. Some concentrated on the legal aspects of the case, some on the point of view of the accused, some on points put forward by the Counsels briefed, some on the Judge's comments and pronouncements.

She entered very few names in the first column, very few in the second, one or two with question marks in the third, and as time wore on and she found no cases at all which fitted her requirements and belonged to both of the first two categories a sense of panic gripped her.

What if she failed after all? What then? She had pinned so much on the hope of success. Doggedly she resisted the temptation to turn the pages too fast. She might miss the one vital fact for which she was searching. Back aching, eyes burning, and with a head-ache increasing in intensity by the minute, she read on.

The record ended about two-thirds of the way through the thick book and the final cuttings had been pasted in in February 1969, shortly before her mother died. She read them dully, with a sense of finality. There was nothing there which remotely resembled what she needed.

With a sense of defeat she turned the last full page and saw that it was stuck to the next at the top. It must have been carefully pasted. She inserted her hand and slid it carefully between the leaves, easing them apart. As they fell open the headlines of the final cutting sprang up at her, thick and tall:

MURDERER VOWS REVENGE

Heart pounding, almost afraid to read on lest the final hope which flared up in her should be extinguished, she leant forward eagerly. The printed words danced and blurred before her tired eyes and impatiently she rubbed at them before she tried again:

MURDERER VOWS REVENGE
A bank clerk was forcibly removed from the Old Bailey yesterday, shouting his intention to revenge himself upon the judge who had just sentenced him to ten years' imprisonment.

Pronouncing sentence, Mr JUSTICE GRAN-THAM told WILLIAM SPRINGER, 29, 'It is the duty of this court to see that human life is protected, and to try to deter people like yourself from destroying it on impulse.'

SAVAGE BLOWS WITH SPADE
Mr MICHAEL HENDERSON, prosecuting, said that on the evening of October 29th, 1968, Springer arrived home from work at 6.50 p.m. to

find his wife somewhat flustered by the persistence of a door-to-door salesman. Springer became very angry with the salesman, THOMAS CRABB, 45, and eventually hit him. Crabb retaliated and was knocked to the ground by Springer, who then seized a garden spade and hit him savagely about the head. Crabb was taken to hospital, but died of his head wounds before arrival.

Mr JULIAN FELLOWS, defending, said that Springer was normally a mild man, whose temper was not easily aroused. His wife, Mabel Springer, to whom he was devoted, was delicate and easily upset, and Springer's attitude towards her was very protective.

AN INTOLERABLE SITUATION

In his summing up Mr Justice Grantham said, 'Unless this sort of thing is strictly controlled the life expectancy of door-to-door salesmen would be no greater than that of test pilots, a situation which you, members of the jury, might regard as quite intolerable.'

Sarah read it through twice, with a soaring sense of excitement. It was tailor-made to her requirements. The motive was clearly there. The man had declared his intention of revenge publicly and violently. And no doubt the years in prison would have confirmed and strengthened it. He had killed to protect his wife in a situation where most men would have been content with words. And in going to prison he had left his wife, towards whom he felt so fiercely protective, defenceless. She might, and Sarah shivered at the thought, she might even have found another protector. That would have fed the man's desire for revenge still further.

He had been given ten years and the newspaper cutting was dated . . . she checked it . . . yes, the same time as the last few others before it, February 1969.

What was the remission for good conduct? One third of the total sentence. So that would make it a sentence of ... her forehead creased in concentration as she worked it out ... about six and a half years. It fitted.

She closed the scrapbook and sat back in her chair, rubbing the back of her neck and flexing her aching back. Looking at the green leather cover of the book as it lay on the table before her, she realized that she had achieved something else this morning: she had exorcized a ghost. For the past couple of hours the book had ceased to be a symbol of pain and rejection, and become simply a means to an end, and had thereby lost its power over her.

She looked at it now with gratitude and ran her finger-tips gently over the smooth, silky surface. A record of part of a man's life, that was what it was, and that man her father. For the first time she was able to think of the book objectively, as the fruit of the love borne by a woman for her husband. She herself had been the innocent victim of that love, she had been ... incidental to it. She realized now that, although she would never be able to forgive her parents for their indifference to her, they had given her one invaluable gift: the knowledge that marriage can last, can be a permanently satisfying relationship.

She remembered her mother, dying of cancer, doggedly going on with this book as if, unable to be a wife in any other way after the long months of pain and confinement to her bed, she was determined to the last to show her husband that she cared.

The last time she had stuck anything into it had been only a couple of days before her death. Sarah had brought the newspapers up to her mother's room, where the woman who lay in the bed was scarcely recognizable as the radiant being she had once been. She had fetched scissors, scrapbook and glue and had held the newspaper up for her mother to see the report.

150

Even the effort to read had been too much for the sick woman, and she had given only a token glance at the paper before nodding to Sarah to cut out the relevant section for her.

Sarah had done so, had applied the glue and laid the cutting in the book in front of her mother, who had moved her hand on to it with painful slowness to stick it in. Then she had shut her eyes and, hand still resting on the scrapbook, had drifted into sleep.

With a jolt Sarah realized that that cutting must have been the one about the Springer case. She wondered suddenly how her father must have felt, sitting on that particular case while his beloved wife lay dying? She opened the book and skimmed through the article again. A man accused of killing another to protect his wife. Could her father, full of anger and despair at the monster of disease killing his own wife, have felt a sympathy with the man in the dock? If that were so, knowing her father, this might well have made him extra harsh in his attitude towards Springer. He would, so to speak, be punishing himself for feeling sympathetic.

Well, she would never know now. With a sigh she closed the scrapbook and gathered up her belongings. She suddenly realized that she was feeling very hungry. She glanced at her watch. It was already a quarter to two. Fresh air and something to eat would do her good. Her mind felt sluggish, over-worked. She had not put so much mental effort into anything for a long time. But it had been worth every minute of the effort. Faced with what she had to show him now, Alec could not refuse to go to the police.

A sudden surge of relief swept over her at the thought and produced a radiant smile for the startled librarian before Sarah pushed her way through the glass doors into the sunlight.

Chapter Fifteen

On the way home Sarah willed herself not to hurry, although every instinct within her was clamouring for haste. She slowed herself down by glancing from time to time at the remnants of the sunset. The sun had sunk below the horizon just as she arrived back at the car park, and over to her right the sky was still luminous with flame, translucent with amber.

Once she had had something to eat and had drunk a reviving cup of coffee, the afternoon had dragged interminably. She had wandered aimlessly round the shops, strolled into the park and watched the children playing, and had eventually drifted in to witness an auction sale.

She was longing to tell Alec what she had found out, and throughout the endless afternoon she had thought of nothing but the Springer case, turning the facts over and over in her mind, trying to estimate what sort of a man he was, seeking to determine her father's attitude from his quoted words and picturing over and over again that dramatic scene in the courtroom when Springer had shouted his threats of revenge.

She had made herself delay setting off for home until she was reasonably sure that Alec would be there before her and she was intensely relieved, as she turned the bend in the lane, to see that there were lights in the house. Even before she was out of the garage Alec had opened the front door and was waiting for her.

'Where on earth have you been?'

'To the library. I didn't want to get home before you did. I'm sorry I'm late. Supper won't be long.' She walked ahead of him into the kitchen.

Alec exploded. 'Never mind supper. I've been worried stiff. I made an effort to get home early and you weren't here.'

'Darling, I've said I'm sorry. I told you, I didn't want to get home before you. I had no idea you'd be here earlier than usual.'

Alec opened his mouth, then closed it again.

'I've been at the library most of the time, and guess what I found out!'

Anger was still making him snappy. 'How on earth should I know?'

'After you'd gone this morning I remembered this.' She took the scrapbook from under her arm.

'What about it?' Alec had seen the book before, had even leafed through it.

'You remember what I was saying last night, about the possibility that one of the criminals my father sentenced might have a grudge against him? I thought I might perhaps find a report of the case in here, so I took it to the County Library to read it through.'

'And did you find anything?'

Sarah glanced at him sharply. She couldn't read his tone. It was neither sarcastic, sceptical, nor genuinely enquiring.

'Yes, look.' And with a flourish she opened the book at the last full page and held it out for him to read.

He read it in silence, with complete concentration. 'It all fits, I must say.'

Brushing aside her disappointment at this lukewarm reaction, Sarah rushed on. 'Of course it does. It fits exactly. The sense of injustice, the grudge, the promise of revenge.' She remembered, briefly, her fear that her father might have been ill-equipped at that particular time to deal with this particular case. 'Even the length of sentence is right. Ten years, minus a possible three and a half for good conduct, brings us to about now.'

Alec calculated rapidly and nodded. 'You're right, it does.'

'So now we'll go to the police, won't we?'

There was a long pause. Incredulously she realized he was still hesitating.

'Alec?'

'I suppose so.'

Conscious of bitter disappointment she cried out, 'But why are you so uncertain? Surely this – ' and she touched the scrapbook, which still lay open at the relevant page – 'is all the proof we need?' Then, as he still did not reply: 'Alec, what are you holding back? There's something you haven't told me, isn't there?' As he shook his head, urgency sharpened her voice still further. 'Yes, there is, I know there is. I can tell. What is it? Please, Alec, tell me. Let's go to the police, please. It never occurred to me that you would still hesitate, after seeing that. Please, let's go. Please. I can't go on any longer.' She was gripping the lapels of his jacket, tugging at them to emphasize what she was saying, willing him to give in to her, directing all the strength of her desperation at him to make him agree.

Gently he put his hands up to hers, eased them away from his jacket and held them tightly. Sarah gazed frantically at him, trying to read his decision, but his eyes were unfathomable, their expression unintelligible to her. There was a hint of sorrow in them as he capitulated.

'All right, Sarah, we'll go.'

She sagged thankfully against him, her strength ebbing away now that the battle was won.

'But,' he continued, and she looked up quickly, fearing what he was going to say, 'not now. Tomorrow.'

154

Then, before she could speak: 'Look, let's go and sit down, and I will tell you what I planned.'

Without answering she allowed herself to be led into the sitting-room. They sat down on the settee and she waited for him to begin.

'You remember Jeremy, Jeremy Taylor? You met him at the wedding.'

Sarah nodded, a spark of hope kindling in her as she realized the significance of the question. Alec's friend Jeremy was a policeman, a detective-inspector to be precise, in the Metropolitan Police Force. She had, as Alec said, met him at the wedding and had not seen him since. Alec occasionally met him in town for lunch, if he had to go up to the Public Records Office, and Jeremy happened to be free. Why hadn't she thought of him before? Alec, though, obviously had, and the knowledge that he had after all been going to do something about her predicament warmed her as she listened. The spark of hope burgeoned.

'I tried to contact him about this business yesterday, but he's been on holiday. They weren't sure if he would be back today, or if he would be staying on for a few days longer. That was why last night I was reluctant to commit myself to going to the police on Saturday. If, for example, I had found that he would be home on Sunday, I thought it would have been much better to wait to see him rather than tell it all to a complete stranger. Anyway, I rang this morning, and he is coming home today. He should be there now, as a matter of fact. He was getting into Heathrow at about three.' Jeremy was still a bachelor and spent any money he could save on exotic holidays.

Sarah felt bewildered. 'But why didn't you tell me all this last night?'

Alec hesitated almost imperceptibly before he replied. 'Because I was afraid you might be disappointed if it didn't come off.'

'That just doesn't make sense. You could see how upset I was last night. Surely you can see that a disappointment like that would have hurt me far less than not understanding why you had changed your mind?'

'Yes, I can see that now.' Alec sounded very contrite, but Sarah was not satisfied. There was still something here that she did not understand, but she couldn't put her finger on it. She said uncertainly, 'There's something else, isn't there?'

'Something else?'

'Some other reason why you didn't tell me.'

'What do you mean?'

'You know perfectly well what I mean. I don't know what it is, but there is something you're not telling me.'

'Sarah, darling, you are imagining things.'

She stood up, suddenly angry. 'Don't "Sarah darling" me. There is something, I know it. There's been something ever since yesterday. Why won't you tell me? I'm sick of all these mysteries and half-truths.'

'Sarah, please, calm down.' He clasped her upper arms, gently but firmly.

'I can't calm down until I know.'

'But there is nothing to know. This business is getting you down, understandably, and you are seeing mysteries where there are none. Look, why don't you sit down quietly on the settee, while I go and ring Jeremy?'

Sarah shook his hands off her arms. 'I don't want to sit quietly on the settee. I'll go and see to supper.' She didn't want to hear what Alec had to say to Jeremy. It was enough to know that at last something constructive was being done towards ending this intolerable situation.

In the kitchen, while her hands automatically busied themselves with preparations for supper, she brooded on her feeling that Alec was keeping something back from her. What could it be? She couldn't think of a

156

single sensible explanation or even, she reflected wryly, any more exotic ones, which was unusual for her.

Alec came in, looking pleased with himself. 'It's all fixed. I'm meeting him at ten.'

'*You* are? What about me?' She could feel the anger rising again.

'Now look – ' Alec was at his most masterful – 'Jeremy could only spare me a quarter of an hour. He has a hectic day tomorrow. You've had an exhausting week, and you are not trailing all the way up to London just for a quarter of an hour's interview. I know all the facts and I promise I won't miss anything out. Later on this evening we'll think of some way of making sure you're not alone tomorrow. Perhaps Mary could come. But you are not going to London with me, and you look so tired now that I think you ought to go straight up to bed. I'll see to supper. No,' he stifled her protests, 'don't argue. Off to bed with you.' He gave her a playful pat on the buttocks.

He was right, of course. Submissively Sarah made her way upstairs. The continual see-saw of emotion which she had experienced during the last few days was certainly the most exhausting and demoralizing experience she had ever had. The short flight of stairs seemed interminable as she mechanically put one foot in front of the other and, hauling on the hand-rail, made her way to the top.

Automatically her feet took her along the landing and paused at the nursery door. Automatically, too, she put up her hand to switch on the light. As the room sprang to life in the sudden glare she was instantly aware that there was something wrong with it. Immediately, like an animal sensing danger, she was tense, alert, her tiredness washed away in a wave of fear. Uncertainly she advanced into the room, step by step, eyes probing into its well-known and well-loved contours.

157

There was nothing wrong that she could see – nothing. She reached the big cot and put out her hands to steady herself by gripping its rails. The much smaller carricot, made up ready for use, lay inside it, and it was as her gaze dropped to this that the nightmare engulfed her. In it lay a mutilated baby.

Chapter Sixteen

She was aware of a high-pitched sound in the distance like the noise of a dentist's drill, boring into every part of her being. She could not associate it with herself, yet a part of her knew that it was herself, screaming.

Suddenly, mercifully, the sound stopped and she realized that Alec's arms were round her, that he was repeating, over and over again, 'Sarah, what's the matter? What is it? Sarah, what's the matter?'

She could not speak, nor look in the direction of the carricot, but her wordless gesture caused Alec momentarily to slacken his hold on her. She felt a frozen stillness in him as he registered its contents, then his grip tightened again, more fierce now.

'Sarah, it's only a doll. Look, there's nothing to be afraid of. Look, it's only a doll, only a doll . . .'

The meaning of his words penetrated her paralysed mind at last and slowly, fearfully, she turned her head, bracing herself in preparation for what she would see.

It was Clementine, her childhood favourite, stripped of her familiar garb, dressed in baby clothes and broken beyond repair. The gaping hole in her china head was the centre of a spider's web of cracks, spreading over the whole of her familiar, beloved face. Her distorted features gazed reproachfully up at Sarah, the macabre effect heightened by the bright red liquid liberally spattered across them.

Full of revulsion Sarah gingerly put out a finger and touched one of the scarlet smears.

'It's paint.'

'I know.' Alec's face was grim.

'But who . . . ?'

'Never mind that for a moment. Let's get you out of here.'

On legs which threatened to buckle beneath her, Sarah walked with Alec's support to their own room, where she submitted wordlessly to being undressed. In her mind was nothing but a terrible blankness and she fought off the successive waves of weariness which threatened to engulf her until she was in bed when, sinking back against the pillows, she surrendered herself voluptuously to them.

The sound of whispering aroused her.

'. . . asleep.'

'Best thing for her.

'But, Doctor . . .'

'No, the best thing, really, I can assure you. She desperately needs a respite, and her body is ensuring that she gets one.'

'Will you wait?'

'No, I'll call back in about an hour, see how she is then.' A pause, then: 'It is essential that I should have a talk with her soon. I think I may have made a wrong decision when you came to see me yesterday morning . . . Mrs Royd?'

At the shock of hearing that Alec had gone to see Dr Blunsdon yesterday, Sarah's eyelids must have flickered and betrayed her. She had decided to remain 'asleep' until the doctor had gone. Resigned, she opened her eyes. There was no point in further pretence. Dr Blunsdon was no fool and would soon find her out once his suspicions were aroused.

His eyes were the little doctor's only sharp feature; all the rest of him was round. With his short, portly

160

figure, chubby face and thinning brown hair he always reminded Sarah irresistibly of her old teddy bear, had the latter worn spectacles. But Dr Blunsdon's spectacles did nothing to detract from the piercing blueness of his eyes, and as Sarah now met his probing gaze she flinched. Not much escaped those eyes.

'Well now, young lady, what have you been up to?'

Sarah didn't reply, couldn't reply. She needed time, to absorb the implications of what she had just heard.

'I'll just take a look at you.'

While she submitted to a brief but thorough examination her mind raced. If Alec had been to see Dr Blunsdon, why hadn't he told her? Was that what he had been holding back? If so, why? She felt, deep down inside her, the first subterranean stirrings of an icy fear, as different from the blinding panic which had gripped her in the nursery as death is from life.

Dr Blunsdon stood up and removed his stethoscope. 'Not much wrong there. Blood pressure up slightly, but not as much as I would have expected. Nothing to worry about anyway. We'll keep an eye on it. And the baby's heart sounds fine. When do you go to the clinic next?'

'Tomorrow morning.'

'Good. I'll give them a ring later on in the morning tomorrow, to see how they find you.' He picked up his bag.

She couldn't let him go like this. She put out her hand. 'No, stop! Please,' she amended.

He raised his eyebrows enquiringly. 'Yes?'

'I heard what you were saying just now. About . . .' She summoned up the resolution to continue. 'About Alec going to see you yesterday.'

There was a long silence. Sarah dared not look at Alec, but she was vividly aware of him, standing motionless beside the bed. Her gaze remained fixed unswervingly on Dr Blunsdon's troubled face. The

161

expression didn't suit him, his features were obviously not accustomed to it. The laughter lines around his mouth and eyes stood out clearly, white against the slight tan he had acquired visiting patients throughout the long, hot summer.

He put down his bag. 'I see.'

Sarah waited. She still dared not look at Alec.

'And you are wondering, of course, about the purpose of that visit?'

She nodded, wordlessly. Her stomach clenched, in apprehension.

He looked at Alec. 'Then I think perhaps it would be better for your husband to explain.'

Unwillingly she transferred her gaze to Alec.

Tension was proclaimed in every angle of his rigid stance, in his clenched fists and troubled eyes. As Sarah watched he suddenly relaxed, as if he had reached a decision. Glancing at Dr Blunsdon as if for reassurance, he sat down on the edge of the bed and took Sarah's hands. 'We – ' and again he looked at the doctor – 'we were hoping it wouldn't be necessary. It was, I suppose, unrealistic of me. After all, it's another three weeks until the baby is due.'

'What has that to do with it? What does it matter how many weeks it is?'

'A lot, I'm afraid.' And again he looked at the doctor.

'What do you mean, you're afraid?' Fear for the child sharpened Sarah's voice and, tugging her hands away from Alec's, she crossed her arms protectively across her stomach.

Alec made a hopeless gesture. 'I'm putting this very badly.'

'For God's sake, Alec, what is it?' She was sitting upright in bed now, terror tightening her muscles and drying her throat.

'Perhaps I'd better continue,' Dr Blunsdon intervened. His hands eased her gently down on to the pillows as he went on: 'Your husband came to see me yesterday because, quite naturally, he was worried about you. He told me that ever since last Friday, when you received the first of those cards, you have been very nervous, very easily upset, liable to lose your temper in a thoroughly uncharacteristic manner. On several occasions he tried to get you to come and see me, but you wouldn't. You would confirm all this, I suppose?'

So Alec had told him everything. Sarah nodded, but did not speak. She knew instinctively that she must conserve every drop of energy for what was coming. Suddenly, she didn't want to know what it was. If Dr Blunsdon had thought it best for her not to know, then it must be best for her to remain in ignorance. She was about to say so, when his next words took her by surprise.

'Have you been worried about anything lately, Mrs Royd?'

She was seized by an almost uncontrollable urge to laugh, to abandon herself to laughter, to drown in it. She suppressed it, with difficulty, and her words came out in a curiously muffled manner. 'Of course I've been worried. Wouldn't you have been, with some maniac pursuing you?'

'I meant, worried about anything else?'

'No, I don't think so.'

'Not, perhaps, about the baby?'

Sarah remembered the frightening periods of panic which had become increasingly frequent over the last few weeks. She hadn't had one since last Friday, it was true, but she could not honestly say that she had not been worried.

'Well, a bit worried from time to time, perhaps.'

'Only a bit?'

'Well, very worried at times, then, if you must know. It's perfectly natural, isn't it?' she continued defensively. 'Mrs Godwin told me that she felt exactly the

163

same when she was expecting Lucy. And she's a very calm sort of person.' Mary was also Dr Blunsdon's patient.

'Yes, of course it's perfectly natural. The only question is one of degree. Just how worried have you been, Mrs Royd?'

She looked at him blankly for a moment, then burst into tears. At once Alec put his arms round her and murmured soothingly in her ear, 'That's it, love, you cry. You'll feel better if you do.'

Although feeling desperately in need of comfort, Sarah pushed him angrily away. 'Sometimes I feel as though I shall never feel better again.'

A peculiar quality in the silence which now fell attracted her attention. She stopped crying abruptly and looked from one man to the other, trying to understand it. Enlightenment burst upon her and she cried out, 'That's it, isn't it? You think my mind is affected? You think . . . my God! . . . you think I've imagined it all?'

She waited for their denials, and when they did not come, she whispered, aghast, 'Imagined it all?' Then, in a burst of desperation: 'But how could I have imagined it? The cards were real. You saw them, Alec, didn't you?' She seized his hand and gripped it fiercely. 'Tell Dr Blunsdon you saw them.' Then, as Alec remained silent: 'And the doll. You saw the doll. Has he seen it?' Frantically she threw back the bed-clothes and started to swing her legs over the side of the bed. 'I'll show you, Doctor.'

Gently but firmly he pushed her legs back on to the bed and covered them up. 'I've seen it, Mrs Royd.'

'Well, then, you must believe me.'

He sighed, hesitated, then went on, 'I do believe that all these things have happened, but not that someone is threatening you.'

She stared at him. 'I don't understand.'

164

'Mrs Royd, let me explain something to you. I will try to be as non-technical as possible. The mind has an automatic defence mechanism against fears which it finds intolerable. For instance, I heard the other day about a little boy who had been very happy at school, and who suddenly started saying that he hated it, that everyone was nasty to him, that he couldn't do the work, that there were a thousand and one reasons why he didn't want to go. The mother approached the head-master, and was bewildered to find that none of this was true. Although the child had been rather with-drawn of late he had plenty of friends, was well liked by the staff and although not brilliant did reasonably well in his work. You are following me?'

He waited for her nod, then continued: 'The head-master was as puzzled as the mother, and decided to approach the Child Guidance Clinic. They discovered that the child's father, who was separated from his mother, had been pestering her to go back to him. The father had always disliked his son intensely, and the boy was terrified that, if his parents were reconciled, his father would persuade his mother to leave him behind. He was afraid to go to school, not because of what he would find there, but because of what might happen while he was away from home. His fear was that he would come home and find his mother gone. But because the thought of her deserting him was some-thing he could not admit even to himself, he detached his fears from the real cause of them, and put them on to his school.'

He paused to give Sarah time to absorb what he had said. 'You do understand what I am saying?'

'Yes, of course I do.' Sarah felt irritated, impatient. 'You are saying that I am so terrified of losing this baby, having had to wait so long for it, that in order to suppress the fear in my mind, I have created another

165

fear, so that I can tell myself that that is what I am afraid of.'

Dr Blunsdon nodded approvingly, as if pleased at the progress of a particularly hard-working pupil.

'I'm sorry, I simply can't believe it. If that were so, who has been sending me the cards? They were real enough. Both Mary and Alec saw them. Didn't you?' she appealed to Alec. 'And who did that?' And she pointed accusingly in the direction of the nursery. A picture of poor Clementine's broken and bloodied face flashed through her mind, and her outflung finger shook.

Dr Blunsdon appeared more ill at ease than at any time since she had woken up. He shuffled his feet slightly on the floor and paused before he answered.

Instinctively Sarah knew that he was not hesitating because he could not refute her argument. It was coming now, she could feel it: the revelation, the heart of the matter, the thing which terrified her. She both shrank from and desired it, dreaded yet longed for it. The fear moved again within her and she could feel herself drawing in upon herself, as a hedgehog curls itself into a tight, impregnable ball when danger threatens. From inside her defences she awaited the enemy.

'It is medically an accepted fact, Mrs Royd, that during pregnancy it is possible for a woman to have black-outs and afterwards to have no memory of what she did during them.' The blue eyes behind the spectacles were filled with pity and apprehension as he awaited her reaction.

Sarah was conscious of a sudden stillness within her, as if time itself were arrested, the stillness of shock and incredulity. The faces of the two men, turned attentively towards her, blurred, lost their shape, then re-focused with exceptional clarity. She became aware of details until then unnoticed: the tiny mole high up

166

on the little doctor's left cheek, the dark ring around the iris of those probing eyes, the length of the lock of brown hair which had flopped down on Alec's bony forehead. I must remind him to go to the barber's, she thought irrelevantly.

Alec cleared his throat uneasily in the silence and the frozen moment dissolved.

Sarah licked her dry lips. 'Are you saying . . .' Her voice came out in an unrecognizable croak and she paused, swallowed hard and tried again. 'Are you saying that I might have done all these things myself?'

The doctor glanced down at his hands, then up at her again. 'I'm afraid so.' His voice was gentle.

Sarah's mind began to move again, sluggishly at first, then faster and faster. It swooped from fact to fact, examining and confirming. This, then, was why, on the one occasion when Alec had been going to call the police, she had argued so vehemently against it, pleading exhaustion; this was why she had repeatedly refused to consult the doctor – subconsciously she knew what she had done, and was afraid of being found out; and this was why, for the last few days, her fears about the baby's birth had completely vanished.

It all fitted together, like a completed jigsaw puzzle, explained away everything which had bewildered her. In the light of this new knowledge, Alec's incomprehensible attitude became understandable, his reluctance to go to the police perfectly logical. Mary's inexplicable change of attitude, too, was now explained; no doubt Alec had rung her yesterday morning, and told her what Dr Blunsdon had said.

Her enemy was the truth.

She had imagined, then, the watcher in the orchard, the figure on the lawn on Sunday night. Hers had been the hands which had cut the cards, carefully printed the threatening messages; it was she who had dressed

Clementine in baby clothes, laid her in the little cot and smashed her head, daubed it with –

'No!'

The vehemence of the monosyllable shattered the waiting silence in the room, and the two men started.

'No. I couldn't have done that to Clementine – my doll,' she explained to Dr Blunsdon's bewildered look. 'I could believe it all, but for that.' Certainty was growing in her, strengthening her. Suddenly she felt trapped, defenceless, vulnerable, lying in bed. It was as if the mere fact that they were standing and mobile while she was not gave them an intolerable advantage over her. Once again she put aside the bed-clothes and swung her feet over the side of the bed. Both men at once moved to restrain her.

'I am quite capable of getting up, thank you.'

They drew back, and she quickly slipped on her dressing-gown, as if it were a mantle of equality. The two men watched her as if mesmerized.

'Shall we go downstairs? It's more comfortable there.' She turned and marched out of the bedroom without waiting to see if they were following, very conscious that the balance of power had shifted, and that it was now she who was in command of the situation.

One part of herself stood aside and watched herself in open-mouthed amazement. Who would ever have believed that she would behave like this, issue orders to Alec and the doctor, take it for granted that she would be obeyed? But then, she had never had to fight for anything so important before. She understood very clearly that she was fighting for her sanity. She could not afford to be weak, to allow the slightest doubt to cloud her certainty. She crushed the little worm of fear that was crawling about somewhere deep down inside her, waited until they were all seated, then turned to the doctor.

'It's a good theory, I must admit. It's very

plausible – ' here she saw him wince slightly – 'but it's not true.

'I loved that doll, you see, more than anything I ever had. I was a very lonely child and she was my friend. I took her everywhere with me, even away to boarding school. I used to worry in case her head got broken. She was a very old doll when I had her, and her head was made of some sort of china. I'm not sure exactly what it was, but it was breakable, unlike the dolls one buys today. I used to take all sorts of precautions against breaking it, especially on long journeys. I would pack her in layers and layers of thick cotton wool, and when we arrived the first thing I would do would be to unpack Clementine and make sure she was all right. I could never have done that – ' and she glanced up at the ceiling – 'for any reason. If I wanted to produce that particular effect I would have mutilated another doll, not Clementine.'

Dr Blunsdon looked unconvinced.

'There is another thing, too,' she went on eagerly. 'Did my husband tell you about the scrapbook?'

The doctor looked puzzled and glanced enquiringly at Alec. 'Scrapbook?'

Before Alec could respond, Sarah hurried on with a brief explanation of her theory. When she had finished she fetched the book from the kitchen and laid it, open, in front of him.

He read it in silence. 'Yes, I see.'

Sarah waited eagerly, but he made no comment, merely closed the book gently and rose. 'I don't think anything will be gained by discussing the matter any further tonight, Mrs Royd. What I would like to do is arrange for you to go into hospital early tomorrow morning, and stay there until the baby is born. Whether I am right or not is irrelevant. The important thing is your welfare, and that of the baby, and I feel that, in the circumstances, hospital would be the safest place.'

For a moment Sarah was sorely tempted. To be safely surrounded by large numbers of people and under medical supervision did indeed seem to be a desirable state of affairs.

'I'm sorry, I couldn't do that.' She was not going into hospital until she had been vindicated, until it had been proved that she was right and he was wrong. The fear that it was the other way about, which still lurked deep down inside her, merely strengthened her determination not to go in until she had proved her point. 'I want to be here when my husband gets back from London. He is going to see a friend of his in the police, to see what he can find out about this man Springer. Aren't you, darling?'

'But even if I do go, I could come and see you in hospital, to tell you what I found out. I think that it would be an excellent idea for you to go in. I'd be a lot happier, knowing you were safe while I was away.'

Sarah noted, but did not comment upon, the 'even if'.

'No, Alec. I want to be able to put this whole wretched business behind me when I go in. Can't we ask Mary to come for the day tomorrow, as you suggested earlier? I'm sure she would.'

'I do wish you would reconsider, Mrs Royd. I would feel a great deal happier if you would.'

'I'm sorry, Doctor, I've made up my mind.'

'In that case, perhaps I can persuade you to go in tomorrow evening, after you have had an opportunity to find out what your husband has learned in London?'

Sarah hesitated. If this theory of hers proved false, it might well be the best, the safest thing to do, until the police had discovered who was really responsible for what had been happening. If, on the other hand, she was right, it would still be better for her to be safely out of the way until Springer was caught. She could always come home again once he was behind bars. 'Yes, all right. On one condition – that you will agree to my coming home again once the man is caught.'

Dr Blunsdon beamed. 'Splendid, splendid. Of course I agree to that.' Clearly he did not believe he would ever be called upon to fulfil his promise. 'Then I will be on my way.'

And amidst polite protestations on both sides he left.

Chapter Seventeen

The shrill, insistent sound bored its way into Sarah's mind through the sleep-laden layers of her consciousness and dragged her into a reluctant wakefulness. The doorbell was ringing, on and on and on, and she stumbled across to the window which overlooked the drive and peered out.

Mary was waiting below, tension and urgency in every line of her stance, as her finger stabbed again and again at the bell.

Sarah fumbled the window open and Mary turned up towards her a face visibly flooded with relief.

'I'll be right down.' Her reactions still slow and movements clumsy, Sarah pulled on her dressing-gown and, snatching up an envelope with her name on it from the bedside table, made her way downstairs.

'What kept you? I was getting really worried.' The anxiety was still there, in Mary's voice.

'Sorry, I was still asleep. What's the time?'

'Ten to nine. I've been ringing the bell for the last ten minutes.'

'I am sorry, Mary.' Sarah led the way into the kitchen. 'I couldn't get to sleep last night. I didn't even hear Alec go. He left a note.' She ripped open the envelope and read the brief message:

Darling,   *8.30*
Just off to London. Won't wake you as you are so sound

asleep. Have a nice day, and take care. Home about 5.30.

> *Love,*
> *Alec.*

She was flooded with relief. He had gone to London after all. The aftermath of the long and bitter argument they had had last night after the doctor had gone was still with her. The tiny germ of fear that Dr Blunsdon could be right, unacknowledged even to herself at that stage, had made Sarah take the uncompromising stand that he was quite wrong, that although she had been worried about the baby she had certainly not been sufficiently anxious for the fear to have the effect he had suggested.

Alec, obviously torn between his anxiety not to upset Sarah further and exasperation that she would not accept what he believed to be the truth, began by being exaggeratedly patient and ended by losing his temper. Sarah's mind still jangled with the accusations they had hurled at each other.

He had eventually agreed, reluctantly, to go to see Jeremy as arranged, and had rung Mary to make sure she would be able to spend the day with Sarah, but his disbelief in the value of such a course of action had been so patent that Sarah had lain awake for hours, wondering if he would go, and turning over and over in her mind the fears and speculations which the events of the evening had triggered off.

It was during those endless, sleepless hours that the doubts had come to torment her. Could Dr Blunsdon be right, after all? Her mind had examined endlessly the arguments for and against his theory, and over and over again she had been forced to the conclusion that she was engaged in a futile exercise, doomed to founder on lack of proof. It was, at the moment, a matter of belief. Alec believed that Dr Blunsdon was right; she believed (or did she?) that he was wrong. Only time could give them the answers. Perhaps, when Alec came home this evening, all this tormenting uncertainty would end. Her spirits rose.

'He says he'll be back at about half-past five.'

'Fine. Look, why don't you go and have a bath and dress while I get you some breakfast? What would you like?' And Mary took the kettle and started to fill it with water.

'That would be lovely. Just toast and coffee, please.'

Her mood of optimism lasted while she bathed, dressed and made the bed, and still buoyed her up when she came down for breakfast. In the kitchen she stood for a moment gazing out of the window before joining Mary at the breakfast table. It was yet another cloudless day, but with an unusual clarity for this hour of the morning. The mists must have cleared away earlier than usual. She had a fleeting image of her enemy, crouched somewhere out there in the dew-drenched grass. She laughed inwardly, thinking how unaware he was that he had been found out, that plans were in hand to thwart him and to splinter his implacable intentions of revenge into a thousand harmless fragments. Today she would be safe, protected by Mary's presence, and this evening she would be safe in hospital while they hunted him down.

'You look very cheerful.' Mary was eating a slice of toast, liberally spread with butter and marmalade. 'Look at all these calories! I know I shouldn't, but it seems an age since I had breakfast.'

'It won't do you any harm, just for once.' Sarah helped herself to toast. 'Yes, I am. Cheerful, that is.' She took a large mouthful and looked expectantly at Mary. 'Aren't you going to ask why?'

Mary contemplated her piece of toast. The words came slowly, reluctantly. 'Why, then?'

'Because I'm sure that today Alec will find out who

is responsible for all that's happened. Did he tell you about the scrapbook, when he rang you last night?'

Mary nodded. 'Look, Sarah, don't you think it might be a good idea to try to forget about it all, for today?' Her eyes came up to meet Sarah's and Sarah flinched. She had seen that look before, in the eyes of both Alec and the doctor. It was compounded of pity, sorrow and distress, and arose from the unshakeable conviction that Dr Blunsdon's theory was true. There was no man to be caught, no criminal with a grudge to apprehend. The only person responsible was Sarah herself, poor deluded creature.

With a hand that shook, Sarah put down the toast, appetite blown away in the icy wind of desolation which swept through her. Bitterness rose like bile in her throat. 'I suppose so.'

'Oh, come on.' Mary rose and came to put an arm around her shoulders. She obviously wasn't prepared to accept capitulation at this price. 'We'll talk about it, if you want to.'

'You're probably right. Better not to.' But she knew she would give in, that she really wanted to talk of nothing else. This one subject obsessed her, possessed her, and all else fell away, dull and insignificant beside it.

Mary gave her shoulder a little shake. Sarah's hurt withdrawal merely made her more determined to persevere, as Sarah had known it would.

'Don't be silly. Show me the scrapbook. Where is it?'

Sarah's pretended reluctance fell away. 'In here, somewhere.' They both looked round. There was no sign of it.

'Perhaps Alec took it to London with him. I'll just go and look in the sitting-room.' Sarah made to rise, but Mary's hand on her shoulder pressed her down.

'No, it's all right. I'm up, I'll go.'

She disappeared into the sitting-room and a moment later Sarah heard an odd sound, something between a gasp and a choke. She rose hastily. 'Mary, what is it?' The fear was there again and she stumbled to the door, knocking a cup from the table in her haste. The small, explosive crash as it smashed upon the floor did not even register on her mind, so much did it blend into the sudden atmosphere of crisis.

Mary was standing in an attitude of frozen disbelief in the centre of the room, staring at the large mirror which hung on the wall opposite the fireplace. The impetus of Sarah's rush into the room carried her a few paces before she, too, stopped dead. Printed scarlet capitals, sprawled across the glass, proclaimed with a certainty which struck terror to Sarah's heart:

THOU FOOL, THIS NIGHT THY SOUL
SHALL BE REQUIRED OF THEE.
                                            LUKE XII.20.

For a few interminable minutes neither of them moved or spoke, then Mary came to Sarah and put an arm protectively around her shoulders. Together they moved towards the mirror. Their twin reflections advanced to meet them, the red letters superimposed across their face. When they stopped the word FOOL hung suspended over Sarah's head, and she looked at it bitterly. Fool indeed, to have thought that this day would bring her any kind of respite. How long had the house been empty, apart from herself, asleep upstairs? Alec's note had been written at eight thirty, Mary had arrived at twenty to nine. Ten minutes, then, and he had seized the opportunity as ruthlessly as he had seized every other which had come his way.

Mary put her finger up to the glass and touched one of the letters. 'Lipstick.'

They avoided each other's eyes. Whose lipstick?

Hers, Sarah's? She crushed the thought that the hand which had used the lipstick might have been her own, and briefly took courage from the fact that he must have been in here while she was still asleep, and had not harmed her. But the comfort of this thought evaporated almost before she had formulated it. The message on the mirror left no room for doubt. Sarah was to be spared until tonight.

Suddenly it was as if a part of her mind detached itself from the Sarah standing as paralysed as a terrified rabbit before the mirror, and saw in one sweeping, objective glance exactly what had been happening over the past week. The whole thing had been a deliberate and carefully executed plan of campaign, building inexorably towards its climax.

First, the printed warning, the first harbinger of fear, followed at carefully planned intervals by others, each more menacing than the last. And, alongside the cards, the purposeful creation of the impression that the watcher was closing in on her; on Saturday and Sunday he had been a shadowy figure, glimpsed from a distance; by Monday he had demonstrated beyond doubt that he was watching her every move from close at hand; by Tuesday he had penetrated into her home, and by Thursday he had shown, viciously, by the mutilation of Clementine, that new locks could not keep him out.

For a moment she glimpsed the intensity of the hatred which lay behind these events. Nothing she had done or could do would deflect him from his purpose. She felt stifled, suffocated, as though the walls of this familiar room were closing in upon her, inch by implacable inch.

She tugged at Mary's arm. 'Mary, let's go out, now, at once.'

Mary nodded but did not speak. Sarah glanced at her sharply. She was staring fixedly at the mirror, her tranquil forehead scored by two sharp vertical lines which Sarah had never seen there before, her lips pressed together and some unreadable, unfathomable expression on her face. Abruptly the planes of her face shifted and resolved into more familiar patterns. 'Where would you like to go?'

Sarah's mind refused to readjust itself to such an immediate, mundane decision, and she stood helplessly, unable to make a single suggestion.

Mary took her arm. 'Let's go, anyway. We can decide when we're out.'

It was not until they were sitting in the car that Sarah remembered that it was Friday, and she had had an appointment at the clinic at nine thirty. It suddenly seemed very important to keep to her usual routine. Deliberately she blanked off the scene in the sitting-room and set off for the hospital. Neither she nor Mary made any reference to what had just occurred. It was dangerous ground, and they instinctively avoided it.

Arriving at the clinic three-quarters of an hour late, Sarah was relieved to find that there were still a number of women waiting and that the reception nurse was too busy to do more than give her a reproachful look and bustle her into a cubicle to undress and be weighed. Emerging with her hospital dressing-gown clutched around her, she was hailed in a piercing whisper by Samantha Allen, waving frantically and looking absurdly childish and out of place amongst the others.

'Wondered if you'd be here today.'

'Hullo, Samantha. How are you?'

'Okay thanks . . . well, better than last time I saw you, anyway.'

And she looked better. Not quite so . . . haunted.

'I done what you said. I told her straight out.'

Sarah racked her brain trying to remember what it was she had told Samantha to do. So much had happened since she had seen her on Wednesday morning that it seemed a lifetime ago instead of just two days.

'Did you?' Perhaps it would emerge.

'Yeah. I said to her, "Look here," I said, "I'm not going to stand for this any more," I said. "You keep your lousy experiences to yourself, or I'm off," I said. "You won't see me around here any more," I said. "With or without the baby," I said. Well, that did it. I babysit for her, you see. My little brother's only seven, and she can't leave him yet. And she does like her good times, dancing and that. And that was it. She stopped. I wish I'd done it before. My Tony told me I should've. I don't know why I don't listen to him.' She shrugged. 'Anyway, there you are.'

'I am glad.'

Samantha edged a little closer. Sarah could feel the bones of her thin elbow through the rough towelling of the hospital dressing-gown. 'Mind you – ' her whisper was almost inaudible and Sarah had to strain to distinguish the words – 'Mind you, I'm still not looking forward to it. When did you say you're due?'

'November the twentieth.'

'Oh, pity.' The pinched face brightened. 'Perhaps I'll be late. If I was a week late, and you was a week early, we'd overlap.'

Sarah laughed. 'You never know.' Then, hastily, seeing the look of hope: 'But I doubt it. We'll just have to wait and see.'

'Mrs Allen.' The nurse had appeared and with a jaunty wave of her hand Samantha was gone, her stick-like legs beneath the dressing-gown looking more pathetically child-like than ever.

When it was Sarah's turn to be examined, it appeared that all was well: her weight was right, her blood pressure only very slightly up ('try to have a good long rest each afternoon, Mrs Royd') the baby's heart was beating strongly and its head neatly engaged.

With a 'We'll see you next week, then', Sarah left. Clearly, if Dr Blunsdon had made any provisional arrangements for her to go into hospital this evening, they had not filtered through to the ante-natal clinic.

She had thought that the day would seem interminable, as had the afternoon of the previous day, when she had been longing to show Alec her discovery in the scrapbook. Now that she was away from the house the trapped, helpless feeling which had come upon her in the sitting-room had faded, and she felt only a vast impatience to know what Alec had found out in London.

But, astonishingly, time flew. After an early lunch they decided to go to see *Snow White*, which was showing at one of the cinemas in the town, some of the schools still being on half-term holiday. Sarah, surrounded by a delighted, boisterous crowd of children, was able to become one of them and to lose herself in the timeless drama of good and evil which unfolded before them. It was only at that supremely terrifying moment when the witch's black-hooded predatory figure completely filled the screen, threatening to engulf the audience in her voracious desire for revenge upon her rival, that she swung, momentarily, back into the reality of her own terror.

When they came out of the cinema they noticed at once the change which had fallen upon the town. The air was still, oppressive, a curious sulphurous light dimmed the bright colours of the women's clothes, the gay wares in the shop windows, and above them a low, spreading bank of cloud had almost blotted out the clear sky which had been with them for so many weeks. The weather was going to break at last.

By the time Sarah had driven Mary to pick Lucy up from the house of a friend, dropped them both at their house and set off finally on the brief journey home, it was clear there was going to be a storm. The bank of cloud, now the colour of lead, stretched menacingly from one horizon to the other, robbing the air of light and movement. Already it was very much darker than it had been the day before at this time.

It was now half-past five and the roads were becoming busier by the minute with the start of the early evening rush home from work. The flare of headlights, switched on early to combat the swiftly approaching darkness, filled the car almost continuously along the main road and it was with a sense of relief that Sarah turned off into the lane which led to their house. She prayed that Alec would be in, and had already decided that, if he were not, and the house was still in darkness, she would not stop but drive straight off again, traffic or no traffic, storm or no storm. She couldn't face the prospect of waiting in the house with that final, deadly promise shouting at her from the mirror in the sitting-room.

So it was with an overwhelming sense of relief that, as she turned the corner by Mr Turner's yard, she saw the house burst upon her in a blaze of light. How very thoughtful of Alec to have turned on every light this time, to have made quite sure that this message of safety and security (and, dared she hope, celebration?) should wait to greet her the moment she came in sight of home. The first drops of rain spattered on to the windscreen as she swung the car into the drive; big, heavy, single drops, forerunners of the deluge to come. Ignoring them, and the first growl of thunder in the distance, Sarah parked by the front door, on which her eyes were fixed. Her imagination brought Alec to it at a run, bursting to tell her the good news, that Jeremy had confirmed her suspicions of Springer, that the situation was now under control.

But the door remained firmly shut. He must be in the kitchen, at the back of the house, and hadn't heard her. Or, she thought, as her fingers fumbled in desperate haste at the lock, perhaps he was in the bathroom – that was at the back of the house too, upstairs.

'Alec?' Her voice, loud in the silence, bounced back at her. She did not wait for an answer but hurried into the kitchen, her gaze raking quickly around the empty room for the tall, familiar figure.

'Alec?' Not so fast up the stairs, of course. Even the urgency she felt to see him, the desperate need to know what he had found out, could not make her heavy body bend to her will and hurry up the stairs as fast as she would have liked.

He must have put on every light in the house, she thought, as she paused at the top of the stairs to get her breath back. Why didn't he reply? She called his name again and hurried along the landing towards their bedroom. So single-mindedly was her whole being focused upon finding Alec that her headlong rush had carried her past the open nursery door and almost as far as the door of their own room before she stopped. Something was wrong.

With the cessation of her own movement the sense of rush and bustle which had invaded the house with her died away to a mere residual whisper and finally to silence. A total silence, yet not dead but alive, expectant, malignant. A low snarl of thunder, closer this time, merely served to emphasize the breathless, waiting quality of the stillness about her. As if sleep-walking, Sarah turned about and took a step towards the nursery door.

Her feet felt nightmare-heavy with the dread of what she should see when she reached it. The world narrowed to the oblong of brighter light set in the landing wall ahead of her. Two steps, three, four. The landing receded behind her as she finally stood in the doorway. It was obvious, now, why Alec hadn't replied.

Chapter Eighteen

Alec hadn't replied because he wasn't here. The blazing lights were a trick, switched on by a malignant hand to dupe her, make her believe that she was safe, lead her joyously unawares into the house and up the stairs and confront her with this.

In the wreckage which lay before her there was not one single item of equipment intact. Her horrified gaze moved over the splintered chest of drawers, the pram with its torn-off hood and mutilated apron, the wooden cot reduced to an unrecognizable jumble of splintered sticks and torn sheets, the ripped carricot and crushed baby chair. And over all, like the first scattering of winter snowflakes, lay the torn baby clothes. Even the walls had not escaped, and the decapitated figures of A. A. Milne's enchanted world stood sentinel over the scene of chaos and destruction spread beneath them.

But the worst thing of all, the thing which struck Sarah like a physical blow, was the force of the hatred which lay implicit in every shattered article in the room. She was aghast, mesmerized by the abnormal strength which had created such havoc, ripped apart wood, canvas, metal as though they were paper.

Where was he now? A sudden clap of thunder almost overhead jerked Sarah out of her frozen immobility. Fear for herself and the baby gripped her and she turned for flight. Her terror too overwhelming for stealth, she ran down the stairs, out of the front door and into the night.

She would never get away on foot, she was too slow. The car was her only chance and as she covered the few paces to where it stood she became aware of the rain, beating down upon her bare head, soaking already through the thin material of her cotton dress. Her hand on the door handle, she paused. The keys. She had left them in the house. She gave a sob of despair. She couldn't go back, she simply couldn't. She turned, brushing wet hair out of her eyes. The house stood silent still. Surely if he had been inside he would have followed her? He wouldn't have risked her escaping him now? Perhaps he wasn't inside after all. Perhaps the time was not yet. Hesitantly she took a step towards the front door. A searing flash of lightning was closely followed by an ear-splitting clap of thunder which made her duck instinctively, shook the front door with the strength of its vibration. Something caught the light streaming from the hall, and with an upsurge of thankfulness Sarah saw that it was her keys, still dangling from the lock. In her haste to get inside, to see Alec, she had forgotten them.

She ran to the door, snatched them out of the lock, then hurried to the car. There was still no sign of pursuit. She wrenched open the door, collapsed on to the driving seat and thrust the key clumsily into the ignition. The engine roared into life and she slammed the car into gear and reversed in a tight circle. She was going to do it, she was going to get away safely! Mechanically she stopped, put the car into first gear.

'Turn right.'

Sarah was at once aware of something cold and hard pressing into her neck.

'Go on, get going. Right.'

As if her hands, her feet, were detached from her will they were moving, instinctively obeying the note of command. The car began to move again, but hesitantly, as if it were not sure of its own mind.

'Windscreen wipers on. And slowly, now. No tricks.' The voice was low-pitched, rasping and completely, chillingly sure of itself.

As if the automatic actions of hands and feet had made her brain start functioning again, instead of the other way about, Sarah began to formulate coherent thoughts once more. The driving mirror showed her nothing but a dark shape obscuring the view through the rear window. There was no street lighting in this lane. It merely wound its way aimlessly through the countryside, passing very few houses indeed and emerging eventually, some four or five miles away, on to another minor road. There was never very much traffic along it and on a night like this, it was very unlikely that they would meet even a solitary car. And even if they did, what good would it do? Nobody was going to stop voluntarily in this weather, and what could she do, anyway, to attract anyone's attention, without the man behind her being fully aware of it?

She became aware of a low, continuous muttering from behind her, monotonous and menacing. She strained to distinguish individual words from the unintelligible stream of sound, to pick out anything which might be useful to her, help her to understand his state of mind, provide her perhaps with a weapon which she could use against him.

As lightning dazzled in the distance, wind tore at the hedges and rain hurled itself against the solid obstacle which was the car, Sarah detached all but a small portion of her mind from the task of driving safely along the narrow winding lane, and focused her attention on the man behind her.

She was gradually rewarded, first by beginning to distinguish the odd word here and there, then by picking out phrases, and finally by understanding most of

185

what she heard. She was helped by the fact that he seemed to be repeating the same thing, over and over again. Got away... revenge... justice... daughter... pay... And, eventually, after the same cycle had been repeated five or six times... 'Thought you'd got away from me, didn't you? Thought you'd escaped by dying while I was still inside. And your fancy wife, too. Thought you were safe, didn't you? Never believed I'd get my revenge, did you?' (He's talking to my father, thought Sarah in horror. Her skin crawled. He's talking to a dead man.) 'Not your idea of justice. Punish an innocent man trying to protect his wife, that's your idea of justice.' (And I was right, thought Sarah. It was Springer all along. And the knowledge was a crumb of comfort to her.) 'Eye for an eye, that's mine. Eye for eye, tooth for tooth, daughter for daughter.' (Daughter for daughter? thought Sarah. What does he mean?) And she warded off panic with difficulty. 'Told you you'd pay – didn't I? – and now you're going to. Thought you'd got away...' And he would begin all over again.

He's mad, mad, insane, thought Sarah. How can one reason with a madman? He was, she realized, steadily whipping himself into a frenzy of hatred, so that when the time came he would be able to fulfil his intentions and destroy her as if she were not a person in her own right at all, but a mere symbol of his revenge.

It was all a nightmare, the rain, the darkness, the storm, the cold, hard steel pressing into her neck, the evil, unseen presence behind her. Such things did not happen to ordinary people like herself. Dr Blunsdon was right. Fear had temporarily unhinged her mind.

'Watch it!' The muttering stopped, and a particularly vicious jab at her neck made her wince, underlining the reality of her situation. One did not feel pain such as this in dreams. The car, which had begun to scrape the bank on the nearside, veered back on to a straight course as she focused her attention once more on her driving.

It was happening, then. And no one could save her but herself. Even if Alec arrived home shortly and, seeing the blaze of lights and the horror of the nursery, realized that she must be in danger, how could he know where she was? She must rely upon herself, pit her wits against those of this maniac. But how? How?

As if the urgency of her thoughts had communicated itself to him, he spoke into her ear. 'Don't think of getting away. You won't.' The flat, unemotional statement chilled her far more than any raving might have done. She could feel his breath on her neck and the sour, rancid smell of it made her feel sick. Instinctively she tried to turn her head away a little to avoid the stench, and at once the pressure of the gun increased.

'I said, don't try anything.'

'I wasn't. I . . .'

'Shut up. Don't talk, either.'

Her neck was beginning to ache from the strain of holding it in the same position, and her fingers, clamped around the steering wheel, were stiff with tension. Consciously she tried to relax a little. She must think of some plan, she must. This journey could not go on forever. Suddenly she saw herself, driving on for ever through the rain-swept darkness, the menacing presence behind her watching over her to eternity with an unremitting vigilance. She would drive on and on and . . . She pulled herself up with a jerk. She must be single-minded, control her imagination, concentrate all her mental resources on finding a solution.

It was hopeless. What solution could there be? Suddenly she felt like a novice at chess, playing a master. This man had all his moves planned out, right to the end of the game.

She thought of the meticulously planned campaign he had waged against her, and of what it had done to her. As the car swished through the runnels of water at the side of the road and the rain-soaked hedges bent to brush it in its passing, anger rose in her, slowly at first, then with a mounting ferocity, driving away the fear, the hopelessness, the certainty of defeat.

This man, this stranger, whom she had not harmed in any way, of whose very existence she had been unaware until yesterday, had disrupted her marriage, damaged her most valued friendship, destroyed the security of her home and extinguished the joy with which she had been waiting for her baby's birth. He had even made her doubt her own sanity. And now he was threatening not only her life, but that of her child. One of the oldest instincts of all – the instinct of a mother to protect her young – came now to Sarah's aid, sharpening her anger and shaping it to a useful tool.

She would win. But how?

The intervals between the flashes of lightning were greater now. The storm was moving away and the rain easing off. The road ahead glistened wetly in the light of the headlamps, and low banks surmounted by hedges still rose up on either side of the road.

Even if she were able to stage an accident or roll out of the car, the hedges would prevent her getting away. It was, in any case, pointless to think of either alternative. The risk of damaging the baby would be too great.

It was hopeless.

On the right the hedge suddenly fell away and a wide, flat grassy verge replaced it. It was at this moment that the engine suddenly started to make a hideous clanking sound. Instinctively, Sarah switched off the engine.

'What are you doing?' Another vicious jab at the back of her neck.

'Nothing. It's the engine. Something's wrong.'

'Switch it on again.'

Sarah turned the key in the ignition. Nothing happened.

He swore, moved the gun so that it was pointing at the side of her head, leaned forward in the gap between the two front seats and impatiently twisted the key himself, without result.

Sarah flinched at the stream of obscenities which poured from him. Obviously this development didn't suit him at all. And immediately came the thought: if it was to his disadvantage, it could be to her advantage. She couldn't see how, yet, but she geared herself up into an even higher pitch of alertness.

Finally he fell silent. Then: 'Get out. Slowly, mind, and no tricks. No bright ideas of running away.' He sniggered. 'I can run faster than you.'

He was right, of course. He could. That was not the way out. And when they were out of the car she stood waiting quietly, breathing in deeply the fresh moist air, seeking to cleanse her nostrils of the taint of him and straining her eyes into the darkness.

Springer reached behind him into the car, fumbled along the dashboard and switched off the headlights, leaving the sidelights on. Now, if any vehicle did pass by, the driver would no doubt think that a courting couple had stopped to make love in privacy.

He grabbed her left arm roughly in his left hand, keeping his right free to hold the gun at her back. 'Right. Start walking.' And he gestured across the road towards the expanse of grass.

She must try to keep him here at all costs. Once they left the road she would be doomed, out of reach of help if it did come. 'Mr Springer . . .'

She sensed the shock that ran through him, as his grip tightened on her arm.

He swung her round to face him. 'How did you know my name?'

He was still only a shape in the darkness, shorter

189

than she had imagined, his face a pale blur. Sarah could have laughed aloud. How could she have overlooked something so obvious? He would think, of course, that he was safe, that there would be nothing to connect him with her.

'We know all about you, Mr Springer. And if I don't get home soon, the police will be hunting for you. So you'd better let me go.'

His fingers dug into her arm. 'But how? How did you know?'

At once she saw the trap which lay in wait for her. She couldn't tell him how she had found out because that would involve mentioning her father and she knew, instinctively, that this was to be avoided. 'I . . . my husband told me,' she lied. 'He has a friend in the police force, who told him they were keeping an eye on you.'

He gave a short, hoarse bark of laughter. 'Not doing very well, are they?'

'But you'll never get away with it, don't you see?' Desperation lent conviction to her voice. 'Once they find I'm missing, they'll know you are responsible.'

He was turning his head, first in one direction then in another, as if trying to decide which way to go.

'Why should I care? And don't talk to me about being responsible. Was your father responsible, to send me to prison for trying to protect my wife?'

He had completely misunderstood her, thought Sarah despairingly, turned the meaning of her threat inside out. No point in trying to defend her father, she could see that. Attempt to exonerate him, then, now Springer had brought him into the conversation?

'But Mr Springer – ' again she saw the outline of his head jerk as she used his name – 'it wasn't my . . . my father who decided . . .' She would have to be very careful how she put it. 'Who decided against you. It was the jury – wasn't it? – all of them together, so . . .'

190

'Don't give me that. You weren't there, were you? He told them what to decide. I heard him, with my own two ears, so don't give me that. I'm not stupid, you know.'

Guiltily Sarah remembered the newspaper account of the trial, her doubts over her father's impartiality at a time when his own wife lay dying by inches. He *should* have been able to detach himself from his domestic situation, keep his professional and private lives completely separate, but even Judges are human and perhaps . . . With an effort she dragged her mind back to the present. This was not the moment to be undecided, to be weak, to leave a gap in her defences. The danger was real, immediate, the enemy here and now, a physical threat to her baby. The time for questioning could come later – if there was going to be a later, she thought hopelessly. She cast about for another approach. Flattery? She had heard that psychotics were vain, and he had just given her an opening.

'Stupid? Of course you're not.' The tone was exactly right, an impatient dismissal of a ridiculous suggestion. 'Anyone can see that. It was obvious from the first,' she said airily, as one intellectual to another, 'that there was an intelligent mind at work behind all that was happening.' Or a cunning one, she thought savagely, a mediocre mind honed to a cutting edge by an insane obsession.

Her eyes, adjusting themselves now to the darkness, were beginning to distinguish the outlines of the man's features: close-cropped dark hair above thick brows and eyes that were black holes in the surrounding greyness of the square face. The hand which still gripped her arm was a channel of communication between them and now she sensed a slight easing of the tension in him, a slackening of the pitch towards which he had worked himself in the car. If only she could keep him talking long enough, perhaps someone might come along. The rain was easing off, and people who would have been waiting for the storm to pass might even now be getting into their cars, starting their engines.

'How on earth did you come to think of a plan like that?' Her conversational tone took for granted that they would discuss the subject further.

'Nothing else to do, was there, but think?' he responded, but the stiffening of the fingers on her arm told her that he had decided what to do, was preparing to move off.

'But how?' she insisted desperately. 'How did you think of it? I would never have thought of a plan like that in a million years.'

To stay or to go? His indecision reached her through the clenching and unclenching of his fingers. He was, clearly, tempted, and tilted his head to one side in a listening gesture. They both waited, scarcely daring to breathe, straining for the sounds of a car. There was nothing, nothing but the restless movement of the hedge branches and the occasional spatter of rain on the roof of the car.

The sense of isolation, the country darkness must have reassured him. The grip on her arm slackened and he relaxed, even leant back against the car. He could not, after all, resist the temptation to boast of his own cleverness.

'It was a laugh, really. I was issued with it, so to speak.'

She was startled momentarily out of her frantic listening for the sound of a car coming along the lane, genuinely intrigued. 'Issued with it?'

She could discern the movement of his lips in the darkness. He was grinning, enjoying the surprise in her voice.

'Yeah. By the prison authorities.' Deliberately he allowed the pause to lengthen, enjoying her bewilderment.

'There was a Bible in my cell – standard issue. One night I knocked it on to the floor by accident. It fell open and a couple of words caught my eye. "Life for life," it said.' He was silent for a moment, remembering. 'And I thought: That's what I'm going to do, when I get out of here. So I read some more. I've never been a reading man, though I managed to scrape through the exams to get into the bank. But after that, it became a sort of hobby, you might say, picking out the suitable bits, sorting them out, choosing the ones which ... which – ' he groped for words – 'which expressed how I felt, about him. A kind of game which wasn't a game, if you get my meaning.' He peered at her in the darkness, as if he really wanted her to understand.

Sarah nodded vigorously, only a fraction of her attention on what he was saying yet sufficiently aware of him to recognize that he needed a response.

'But the real part, the planning how I'd use them, didn't come till later, until after ... after ...' Abruptly, shockingly, he was alert, upright, his fingers digging painfully into her arm.

'After what?' cried Sarah, caught unawares, so sudden and unexpected had been the reversal of his mood.

'Never mind. We've wasted enough time. Move.' His voice was rough again, harsh with some emotion beyond her comprehension, and as he began to propel her across the road his other hand came up to press the gun into her back.

As she stumbled over the edge of the wide grass verge a last flash of lightning in the distance momentarily illuminated what lay before them. She recognized, instantly, where they were. The area of grass fell away, after a few paces becoming a gentle slope which flattened out into one of the area's favourite picnic spots, a wide grassy bank running alongside the river. Sarah and Alec had been here often in the summertime and

193

she felt a tremendous surge of joy as she realized that, in causing her car to break down at this one particular spot, fate had provided her with a weapon at last.

As they moved together towards the river bank her mind raced ahead, planning. She would need just one moment, one split second in which Springer's attention must be distracted, turned away from her. Please, God, let me think of something! she prayed.

It was as they reached the flat area at the side of the water that they both became aware of a new element in the situation. Sarah, intent on her plan, did not notice it until Springer's grip on her arm, reaching vice-like proportions, drew her attention to it.

A car was approaching at speed, from the direction in which they had come. The roar of the engine, faint at first, became louder and louder and they both swivelled their heads to watch its approach. The glare of its headlights swung and dipped as it wound along the lane towards them, obscured until the last moment by the high hedges which stopped abruptly on this side of the road as it curved to run alongside the river.

There was nowhere to hide, nowhere to take cover, and the headlights flared briefly over them as the car swung around the last bend. Then there was a squeal of brakes as it screeched to a halt beside Sarah's car.

'Sarah!'

Her assailant released her arm and swung away from her in shock towards the sound of the voice. This was the moment she had been praying for. Any second now he would turn and shoot her before it was too late. She could not risk waiting for Alec to reach them. And all fear and despair, the bewilderment and misery of the past week, boiled up in her to a white-hot, searing anger as she thrust out her hands, gave him one mighty push, and then dived herself into the river.

The shock of the icy water took her breath away, but she kicked off her shoes and forced herself to stay under water until her lungs were bursting, striking out with long, powerful strokes for the centre of the river. She did not know if he had gone into the water with her, but she was not going to risk surfacing within shooting distance of the bank.

When she came up for air, sucking great healing breaths into her straining lungs, it was impossible to see if he was still there or not. But if she could not see him on the bank, then he would surely not be able to see her in the river and she trod water, straining to catch the slightest sound, conscious of the icy chill that was creeping over her. She wouldn't be able to wait much longer.

'Sarah? Sarah?' There was desperation in the voice.

In the surge of relief which overwhelmed her it was a moment before she could find sufficient breath to answer. 'Alec. I'm coming.' If Alec were there and calling for her, it must be safe, and she set off for the bank, swimming more slowly now and becoming conscious of a rapidly increasing feeling of weakness now that the crisis was past.

It was as Alec was helping her up on to the bank that the first contraction gripped her.

Chapter Nineteen

She was a mechanism for breathing, nothing more. Her awareness was focused totally on the speed and rhythm of the air moving in and out between her parted lips, through her nostrils. In between the contractions she did not exist; she lived only in those short, concentrated minutes when, summoning up the last tattered remnants of energy which remained to her, her mind and body fused in their unity of purpose.

In that moment, twelve hours before, when she had lain, gasping like a stranded fish on the river bank, it did not seem possible that any reserves of energy remained to her. When she had felt that first vibration at the base of her belly, a sensation never felt before but in some strange atavistic way immediately recognizable, she had thought: Oh no, not now. It can't be. I can't face it now, not like this. And then, as time went by and the pattern emerged: But it's not fair, not fair. Not after her experiences of the last hour, which had tapped sources of determination and courage she had never known she possessed, and which had left her drained of resolution and energy.

Alec had wrapped her in his coat, carried her to the car and driven straight to the hospital. Neither of them had spoken. There was too much to say, and no time in which to say it. Explanations, recriminations, apologies, could wait.

Received by sympathetic nurses, who hid their

incredulity at her condition as best they could, she had moved in a dream through the routine of admission, focusing on reality only during contractions, gathering strength in the intervals for the more difficult hours ahead.

And now she was nearly at the end of her strength. Her resources had been too severely tried, the demands on them had been too violent, too protracted.

They had let Alec stay with her throughout, and the knowledge that he had done so despite his deeply felt reluctance had, in the early stages, helped. But now, in this impossibly long transition stage, when every fibre of her being was longing to push, to rid her body of this burden which was making such intolerable demands upon it, she knew that she had been driven too far, that the limits of her endurance had been passed long ago, that she was going to fail.

She lay now, eyes closed, arms at her sides, fingers limply curling from palms upturned, waiting for the next contraction, that passion of vibration which possessed her labouring womb in the effort to cast forth into the world the life within. Dimly she was conscious of a nurse examining her, but she had been too often disappointed to ask again, 'Can I push, now?' That moment would never come, and if it did, she would not be here to greet it, she would be gone, floating free and weightless away from the impossibility of finding the energy she would need.

'Mrs Royd. You can push now, Mrs Royd. Come along, one last effort.'

Hands eased her up a little more on the pillows, insistent voices begged her, coaxed her, demanded from her that she should push. And, from one last, hidden recess within her came, incredibly, the strength. With the next contraction she bore down with every last fibre of her being, and almost at once there came a sense of release so great that she felt as though she were drowning in it. And then, miraculously, came the cry. Even before the whole of the child's body was exposed for the first time to the harsh winds of reality, its thin wail announced that a living being was entering the world.

In a few moments it was over. And, at last, the words which had echoed through Sarah's mind times without number were spoken.

'It's a girl, Mrs Royd. A perfect little girl!'

Perfect. But Sarah could wait no longer. Released at last from obligation, fear and hope, she drifted away into the comforting darkness, where nothing would be asked of her, no emotion would be felt, and her exhausted mind and body would be free to gather strength untrammelled.

She awoke to dimmed lights, humped shapes about her in the neighbouring beds, and a sense of incredulity. Had it really happened, or had it all been a dream? Her hands moved down to her flat, unfamiliar belly. And the baby? Frantically she pressed the bell-button at the head of the bed.

It was some minutes before a harassed nurse appeared.

'My baby. Can I see her?'

The nurse sighed. 'Look, we're short-staffed, there're two women in the labour wards and the babies are due to be fed shortly.'

'Please. I haven't seen her. I . . .'

'Look, Mrs . . .'

'Royd.'

'Mrs Royd?' The nurse's expression changed, and she looked curiously at Sarah. 'Just a moment, please.' And she was gone, her shoes tapping away across the shadowy wastes of the silent ward.

Sarah waited tensely, her fingers gripping the sheets. Why had the nurse looked at her like that? Something was wrong. It had all been a dream after all. Her mind refused to formulate the horrifying possibilities and she focused every ounce of her attention on the glass doors at the end of the ward, through which the nurse had disappeared.

They swung open again and she re-entered, this time carrying a pink-wrapped bundle. Scarcely daring to breathe or hope, Sarah's eyes fastened hungrily upon it.

'Here she is.' The bundle was handed over, and for the first time Sarah looked at the tiny, crumpled, flower-like face of her sleeping daughter.

'Your husband's still here. He's been here all day, I understand. He wouldn't leave until you woke. I'm afraid you can't see him now, but I'll tell him you are awake and have seen the baby.'

Sarah smiled acquiescence. Of course, that would have been why the nurse had looked at her so oddly. She would have been told about Sarah's condition when she had been brought in. She couldn't have been on duty the night before, or she would have remembered, but no doubt she had heard all about it from her colleagues. She gave herself up to the pleasure of studying the baby. In wonder she folded back the blanket, studied the minute, perfectly formed limbs, marvelled over the minuscule fingers and toes, then, carefully re-wrapping the blanket around the tiny body, lay back against the pillows. As the joy and relief welled up in her she felt that never again could she hope to attain such sheer, unadulterated happiness. Here, at last, was the child she had longed for, the fruit not only of her love for Alec, but of her, Sarah's, personal victory over circumstances so adverse as to have seemed invincible. Not only had she achieved the miracle of a painless birth, she had done so against impossible odds, and with her reserves of strength depleted beyond belief.

Her mind shied away from the thought of that drive

through the night and its climax. Such thoughts were not for now, when the purity of the baby in her arms precluded all that was dark and evil from her mind. This moment of sweetness was too valuable to be wasted, and it was enough that it was here to be savoured.

Relinquishing the baby reluctantly to the nurse, she slid down in the bed, stretching luxuriously, testing the new lightness of her body. She felt, for the first time in her life, strong, free and confident. Brimming over with heady exultation, she almost laughed aloud with delight. The poor, pale shadow of a Sarah had gone and she, new-born as the baby she had held so recently in her arms, was alive as she had never been before.

Chapter Twenty

By the following afternoon, however, sitting up in bed waiting for visiting time, Sarah found that it was not enough merely to exult in her present situation, to revel in the delicious novelty of admiring her tiny daughter. Alec had been allowed to see her for just a few moments in the morning, but there had been time only for the briefest exchange of platitudes.

Apart from the fact that she was bursting with questions, she had been thinking long and hard about Alec, about herself, about the effect which the events of the past week would have upon them. The old balance between them was gone for ever, she knew that. Too much had happened, she had changed too much for their relationship to remain unaltered. There was within her now an inner core of certainty, of self-confidence and self-respect which had never been there before. She had been tested, and had not been found wanting. The knowledge warmed her in some ways, frightened her in others. She was especially uneasy as to how it would affect her relationship with Alec.

And what about Alec? What effect might the events of the past week have had upon him? How would he react to the knowledge that he had failed her, that if he had believed her and gone to the police earlier she would have been spared so much unhappiness and danger? Would he blame himself, or would he be on the defensive, make excuses for himself? She could not bear it if it were the latter, for this would mean that he was not strong enough to shoulder blame, to accuse himself and accept his guilt. Inevitably he would be diminished in her eyes, and how could she live with someone she did not respect?

Her feelings towards him were, in any case, very mixed. Resentment and anger over his failure to believe her, relief at his appearance at that crucial moment on the river bank, gratitude for having stayed with her throughout her labour, were all jumbled up together, and she felt that much would depend upon his attitude when she saw him.

Fortunately, as it was Sunday, she would not have to wait until the evening, and she watched the hands of the clock moving towards half-past two with a mixture of eagerness and apprehension.

There was a sudden flurry of activity as the doors of the ward opened to admit two nurses wheeling a bed-trolley loaded with a new patient and all the paraphernalia of a stay in hospital. A third nurse followed, pushing one of the tiny metal cots on wheels in which the babies slept. There was nothing unusual in this. As babies were delivered and new entrants were admitted to the pre-labour ward downstairs, those mothers who had had their babies were transferred to the mother and baby wards upstairs. There must have been a last-minute admission, and the nurses were hurrying to complete the transfer before visiting time.

There was an empty bed next to Sarah and as the small entourage approached she was surprised and delighted to see the face of little Samantha Allen beaming at her from the trolley. The nurses expertly transferred the girl to the vacant bed, stowed away her possessions in the locker and hurried away. The moment they had gone Samantha leaned across.

'We're in together after all, then. I asked downstairs, and they told me you was here. Got a girl, they said.'

Dutifully she raised herself up to peep at Sarah's baby, sleeping peacefully in her trolley. 'What are you going to call her?'

'Ruth,' Sarah was touched by the girl's politeness. Samantha was clearly bursting with pride and longing to mention her own baby. 'What did you have?'

'A boy. Jason, we're going to call him.'

Sarah craned to see the soft, dark down on the top of his head, which was all that was visible of Jason. 'He's beautiful.'

'I can't believe I've done it! Seven pounds, he is, and it wasn't so bad, thanks to you. I kept telling myself I could do it, and remembering what you said, and it was all right. Till just before the end, anyway.' The small features pinched at the memory, then brightened again. 'And then it wasn't too long until he came, so it didn't matter.'

'I am glad.' Sarah was delighted, for her own sake, as well as for Samantha's. It had not been too late, after all. She had been able to help. 'Thanks to you,' Samantha had said, and 'remembering what you said.' She could not remember anyone ever having said such a thing to her before, except over the most trivial matters.

Perhaps, she thought, it had been the extremity of her own need which had made her more aware of Samantha's – and of Angela's, too, she realized. Perhaps in some topsy-turvy fashion, she ought to be grateful to Springer, not only for making her depend upon herself, for once, but for shocking her out of her self-preoccupation into a new perspective. The very real threat against herself and her baby had made her see how much of positive value there was in her life. She realized, shaken, that the self-pity which had until then been her constant companion for as long as she could remember had crippled her and made her incapable of being of any real use to anyone. From now on, she vowed fiercely, she would be different.

'There's my Tony!' Samantha let out a squawk which made Sarah jump and earned her a disapproving glance from the ward sister, standing by the now open glass doors.

And here, too, was Alec.

'How are you?' He bent to kiss her.

'Fine, thank you.'

His face lightened as he bent over the cot and touched the tiny tuft of dark hair with the tip of one finger. 'I still can't believe it.'

'Neither can I.'

He drew a chair close to the head of the bed and sat down. In this position he was slightly lower than Sarah as she sat propped up against the pillows on the high bed and she gazed for a moment absorbing this unfamiliar view of him. With a twinge of concern she noted the dark smudges beneath his eyes, the deep vertical creases between the dark brows.

'You look tired.'

'I'm fine.' He brushed her concern aside impatiently. 'Are you sure you're all right?'

'Of course.' Now it was her turn to be impatient. 'Alec – ' she leaned closer to him – 'how did you find me, on Friday night?'

'As I turned the bend by Turner's yard I caught a brief glimpse of what I thought was your car, just disappearing around the next bend. I thought that it couldn't possibly be you, as the house was blazing with lights, but when I saw that your car wasn't in the garage, I was worried, naturally.

'I left my car in the drive and dashed indoors, calling you. When I saw the nursery – ' their eyes met, briefly, and flinched away from each other at the memory – 'I guessed that the car must have been yours, and rushed off after you.'

They were both silent, re-living those frantic moments.

'What about you?'

Briefly, she told him what had happened. 'What became of Springer, afterwards? What did Jeremy tell you about him?'

'Well, when I saw Jeremy it didn't take him long to find out that it was more than likely you were right. Springer had been released from prison with full remission for good conduct, three weeks ago. The police have discovered, since, that he has been staying at the *Dog and Duck* in Barton since Wednesday of last week. The landlord recognized his photograph. Apparently Springer said he was on holiday, and used to go off on his motor-cycle in the morning, and come back in time for supper. On Sunday night he didn't come back until the early hours – the landlord was furious; because Springer was so late he had assumed he wasn't coming back at all that night, and he had to get up to let him in. That would have been the night you saw him on the lawn. The police found his motor-cycle in the hedge a few hundred yards away from the house, covered over with branches. Apart from that, he seems to have made no attempt to hide the fact that he was in the area. He took good care not to be seen near our house, of course, but he seems to have assumed that, as there was no apparent reason to connect him with you, he had no reason not to stay quite openly in Barton.'

'Did you find out anything else about him – I mean, apart from what he had been doing for the past week?'

Alec hesitated.

'Did you? Please, Alec, I need to know.'

'I didn't want to distress you. God knows, you've had enough to put up with over the last few days.'

'I'd rather hear it all now, and be done with it. Otherwise I shall just lie here wondering and speculating. You must see that.'

'I suppose so. Well, apparently, while Springer was in prison, his wife and daughter were killed in a train crash. When he was told he went berserk, attacked the governor, who had broken the news to him, and smashed everything he could lay his hands on. He ranted and raved until he was exhausted, shouting that it was all your father's fault, that if he hadn't been in prison it would never have happened, his wife and daughter would never have been on that train, they never went anywhere without him and he always took them by car. He almost lost his remission for good conduct, but the prison authorities decided to be lenient in the circumstances and his outburst was overlooked. Apart from that one occasion, he was a model prisoner.'

Springer's rasping voice was in her head, drowning Alec's words. 'The planning didn't come till later,' he had said. 'Until after . . . after . . .' And then there had been that sudden change of mood, from boasting reminiscence to vicious single-mindedness. This, then, the death of his wife and child, had been the final blow which had changed fantasy into deadly intention, shaped the ruthlessness with which he had pursued her. Suddenly she was back in the car, forging through the wet and windy darkness. 'Your daughter for mine . . . daughter for daughter,' he had said. Easy, now, to understand why, when he had found out that Sarah's father was dead, he had transferred his plan of revenge to her. She shuddered and gripped Alec's hand. 'I see.'

'What's the matter? What do you see?'

'In the car, Springer kept on muttering.' Again she shuddered at the memory. 'It was horrible. "Daughter for daughter," he said, over and over again, "your daughter for mine." He was talking to my father, you see.'

'Don't dwell on it, love, it's all over now.'

'I know, but I can't help it. How old was she, his little girl?'

'Four, I think.'

'Only four? Just a baby, really.' They both glanced instinctively towards the cot. 'Poor man.'

'Don't feel too sorry for him, darling. You mustn't forget that he began it all himself by killing an innocent man.'

'I know that.' Sarah saw again the destruction in the nursery, understanding now that she had partially misinterpreted the feeling behind it. It had not been hate alone, but despair, and the raging frustration of impotence in the face of the blows which fate had dealt him, which had lent that abnormal strength to Springer's arm. Perhaps, even then, he had known that killing Sarah would not ease his burden, perhaps the act of destruction had really been aimed at himself, the instigator of the whole chain of events. A man picked up a spade, she thought, and three people died. 'What will happen to him now?'

'I'm not sure.'

Some reservation in Alec's voice made her look sharply at him. 'Alec, what is it?'

'What do you mean?'

'Surely he didn't get away with it?' Her new-found peace ebbed away. The thought that her tormentor might still be at large, able to pursue her yet, constricted her throat and dampened the palms of her hands with the sweat of fear.

'We don't think so.'

'What do you mean, you don't think so?' Alarm raised the pitch of her voice. 'Don't you know?'

'Shh.' He glanced around uneasily, and hesitated. 'He . . . went into the river, as you know.' He paused again, then took Sarah's hand. 'They have found out, since, that . . . he couldn't swim.'

Sarah stared at him in silence, taking in the implications.

Alec gave her hand a little shake. 'Don't look like that, Sarah. We don't know yet, for sure. They are still dragging the river. And he hurried on, 'in any case, you mustn't blame yourself, there's no blame attached to you.'

'How can you say that?' The effort of keeping her voice down strangled her and it came out in a choked whisper.

'Because it's true.' He shook her hand again, fiercely. 'You must believe that.'

'How can I believe it? I am responsible, of course I am. I pushed him. I didn't know he couldn't swim.' A strong swimmer herself, the possibility had, quite simply, never occurred to her.

'How could you have known?'

'And they are still looking for him, you say?'

Alec nodded. 'Yes.'

'But it's nearly two days now.'

'I know. Look, Sarah, if the man is dead, you really must not blame yourself. No one else blames you. I'm afraid that you'll have to answer some questions of course, but the police have been very understanding. Knowing all that you've been through, and in view of the fact that they still haven't found him, they agreed not to take your statement until you had recovered a little and I'd had a chance to talk to you.'

Sarah found, to her astonishment, that she no longer had any clear idea of what she would tell the police. Before, it had all been crystal-clear to her, but now she felt hopelessly confused – guilty at having sent Springer to his death yet full of valid reasons why she had no choice in the matter, relieved that she need never be afraid of him again, yet conscious of a strange pity for the man who had caused her so much suffering. Had he known, at the last, that his meticulously planned revenge could not purge him of his unhappiness? And had he, in the light of that knowledge, welcomed the dark oblivion of the river, gone willingly to meet his death, believing that it would bring him a peace he could never find alive? Or were such thoughts merely a convenient means of deluding herself into thinking that it had all been for the best, of mitigating her guilt?

'They've found him.'

Sarah had been so absorbed that she had not seen the approach of the nurse with the small slip of paper which Alec now handed to her:

Springer's body found in river at Barton Weir.

J.T.

She read it, then handed it back to Alec. It was over, then, finished.

'Will they let you stay with me, while I give my statement?'

'I don't know. I don't see why not.' He looked away from her. 'It won't be a particularly pleasant experience for me, you know.'

'For you? Why not?'

'I don't come too well out of this. The man who stood by and did nothing, while his wife was hounded by a homicidal maniac.'

The depth of his bitterness, the virulence of his self-recrimination shocked her. She looked at his bent head, bowed back, clenched hands, and realized, shaken, that whereas her self-confidence had been immeasurably strengthened by what had happened, his had been perhaps irreparably damaged.

She saw, too, that it was she who had made him vulnerable to this degree by believing him to be infallible, stronger than he really was, so that when his fallibility was laid bare and his weakness revealed he felt himself diminished not only in his own eyes but in hers.

'Don't say that. It's not true. If you hadn't come after me, been there at the critical moment, I would never have had the chance to get away.'

Alec, clearly unconvinced, said nothing, did not even raise his head.

'I mean it, Alec.' For a moment she was there on the river bank in the darkness, the gun pressed into her back. 'You distracted him, at just the right moment.'

'But if I had acted earlier, you need never have been there in the first place.'

'And,' she pressed on, 'if you hadn't stayed with me all those hours while I was in labour, I would never have found the strength. I would have given up. I knew that you hadn't wanted to be there, that you were doing it for me. I would never have managed without you.' She had to convince him, for her own sake as well as his. She saw now that she had been deceiving herself. However much confidence she might have gained, however much insight into her own strengths and weaknesses she might have achieved, she would never be self-sufficient. She needed to lean on Alec, would always need to lean on him, and for that he must be strong and whole, his belief in himself unimpaired.

'It's no good, Sarah, you can't argue away the fact that if I had listened to you and believed you as I should have, the course of events would have been very different.'

'There's something I haven't told you.'

Alec's head came up with a jerk at the gravity in her voice.

'Why do you think I argued so strongly against Dr Blunsdon's idea?'

'Presumably because you knew that he was wrong.'

Sarah shook her head. 'No, because I was afraid he was right.'

'You believed him?'

'Almost. It was so terrifyingly reasonable. It explained everything so neatly that it almost had to be true. And I was so frightened that it was, that I might be losing my sanity, that I dared not admit the possibility to anyone, not even to myself. Oh, don't you see, Alec, that if I was afraid, myself, that it might be true, you can't be blamed for believing it?'

'You were afraid that it might be?'

Sarah nodded.

He took both her hands in his. 'Poor darling. It must have been hell.'

She sagged back against the pillows. She had done it. Sympathy comes, usually, from a position of strength. Alec would no doubt need further assistance, might not yet be fully convinced, but she would make sure that he was, in the end.

He would call the tune again, and she would dance. That was the way she wanted it.

LAST SEEN ALIVE
Dorothy Simpson

It was all of twenty years since Alicia Parnell last saw Sturrenden. While she was still a schoolgirl a jilted boyfriend had killed himself, and her parents had tactfully moved away from that corner of Kent. Nevertheless the old crowd were delighted to welcome her when she turned up out of the blue one day. Just why she'd come back, though, no one could guess.

But within hours Alicia was found strangled in her room at the Black Swan. And for Inspector Thanet – who had known all of them since his youth – there were special problems. Could he have lived most of h is life alongside someone who harboured a grudge so strong that only Alicia's death could settle the matter? Or would his investigations turn up fresh scandals, a murky undercurrent to life in that placid old market town of which even he had been blissfully – and tragically – ignorant?

'A seamless crime story that offers a startling and believable surprise ending'
Publishers Weekly

'Well organised . . . a cunningly contrived plot'
TLS

0 7221 7877 8
CRIME

DEAD BY MORNING

Dorothy Simpson

On a snowy, February morning, Leo Martindale is found
dead in a ditch outside the gates of his ancestral home –
apparently a hit and run victim.

After an absence – and a silence – of twenty-five years, he
had just returned to Kent to claim his vast inheritance. Is
his death an accident? Or is it, as Inspector Thanet of
Sturrenden CID begins to suspect, murder?

As his investigation proceeds, Thanet finds a profusion of
suspects – all glad to see the last of Leo Martindale, and
more importantly, all with opportunity to kill him. In a fog
of conflicting suspicions, Inspector Thanet struggles to
solve one of his toughest cases . . .

'Well-rounded characters, a satisfying mind-teaser, the
best of British'
The Observer

0 7474 0549 2
CRIME

SUSPICIOUS DEATH
Dorothy Simpson

ACCIDENT, SUICIDE ... OR MURDER?

The woman in the blue sequinned cocktail dress was
dragged from her watery grave beneath a bridge. A highly
suspicious death – and Inspector Thanet is called in to
investigate.

The more he learns about the late Marcia Salden, mistress
of Telford Green Manor, the less likely a candidate she
seemed for suicide. A successful self-made woman with a
thriving business, she had everything she wanted,
including the mansion she had coveted since childhood.
She also had a knack for stirring up trouble ...

As Inspector Thanet attempts to unravel the complex
sequence of events surrounding her death, he discovers
that if Mrs Salden hadn't managed to get herself
murdered, it wasn't for want of trying ...

0 7474 0128 4
CRIME

☐	DOOMED TO DIE	DOROTHY SIMPSON	£3.99
☐	SIX FEET UNDER	DOROTHY SIMPSON	£3.99
☐	THE NIGHT SHE DIED	DOROTHY SIMPSON	£3.99
☐	PUPPET FOR A CORPSE	DOROTHY SIMPSON	£3.50
☐	CLOSE HER EYES	DOROTHY SIMPSON	£3.99
☐	DEAD ON ARRIVAL	DOROTHY SIMPSON	£3.50
☐	ELEMENT OF DOUBT	DOROTHY SIMPSON	£3.50
☐	SUSPICIOUS DEATH	DOROTHY SIMPSON	£3.99
☐	DEAD BY MORNING	DOROTHY SIMPSON	£3.50
☐	LAST SEEN ALIVE	DOROTHY SIMPSON	£3.99

Warner Futura now offers an exciting range of quality titles by both established and new authors. All of the books in this series are available from:

Little, Brown and Company (UK) Limited,
Cash Sales Department,
P.O. Box 11,
Falmouth,
Cornwall TR10 9EN.

Alternatively you may fax your order to the above address. Fax No. 0326 376423.

Payments can be made as follows: cheque, postal order (payable to Little, Brown and Company) or by credit cards, Visa/Access. Do not send cash or currency. UK customers and B.F.P.O. please allow £1.00 for postage and packing for the first book, plus 50p for the second book, plus 30p for each additional book up to a maximum charge of £3.00 (7 books plus).

Overseas customers including Ireland, please allow £2.00 for postage and packing for the first book, plus £1.00 for the second book, plus 50p for each additional book.

NAME (Block Letters) ....

ADDRESS ....

....

☐ I enclose my remittance for _____

☐ I wish to pay by Access/Visa Card

Number ☐☐☐☐☐☐☐☐☐☐☐☐☐☐☐☐☐☐

Card Expiry Date ☐☐☐☐